PRAISE FOR

# *Timekeeper*

"This book was a quick and fun read filled with romantic suspense and mystery. Alexandra makes her heroes so swoon-worthy."

*–Happily Ever After, USA Today (blog)*

"The sheer desperation of Michele's quest to reunite with Philip is compelling. The setting–Manhattan, both turn of the century and contemporary–stands out clearly as the true centerpiece of this love letter to the opulence of the Gilded Age." *–Booklist*

"*Timekeeper* is a delicious treat to readers who enjoy a good dose of history, a craving for mystery and an appetite for a good structured story." *–The Solitary Bookworm*

"This sequel to *Timeless* delivers plenty of romance with even more time-traveling excitement." *–Kirkus Reviews*

# Timekeeper

## ALEXANDRA MONIR

EMBER

Visit us on the Web! randomhouseteens.com
Educators and librarians, for a variety of teaching tools, visit us at
RHTeachersLibrarians.com

The Library of Congress has cataloged the hardcover edition of this work as follows:
Monir, Alexandra.
Timekeeper / Alexandra Monir. — 1st ed.      p. cm.
Summary: Bewildered by a new student at her Manhattan high school who does not know her but seems to be Philip Walker, her lost love from her time travels, and threatened by Rebecca, who has held a grudge against her family for 120 years, sixteen-year-old Michele Windsor seeks help in her father's journals and The Handbook of the Time Society.
ISBN 978-0-385-73840-8 (hardback) — ISBN 978-0-375-89413-8 (ebook)
[1. Time travel—Fiction. 2. Love—Fiction. 3. Revenge—Fiction. 4. Wealth—Fiction. 5. Social classes—Fiction. 6. Families—Fiction. 7. New York (N.Y.)—Fiction. 8. New York (N.Y.)—History—1898–1951—Fiction.]   I. Title.
PZ7.M7495Thm 2012      [Fic]—dc23      2012016869

ISBN 978-0-385-73841-5 (tr. pbk.)

Printed in the United States of America
10  9  8  7  6  5  4  3  2  1
First Ember Edition 2014

Dedicated to my amazing father,
who I would gladly travel back in Time for.
Shon Saleh, thank you so much
for all of your love, support, knowledge,
and inspiration.
I'm so lucky to be your daughter!

Time may be the master of most human beings, but yours is a body and soul it cannot conquer. This unshakeable, undisputed force, which turns day into night and infants into elders, keeps its inner workings and phenomena under a mostly impenetrable veil. If you are reading this, then you have been chosen to lift the curtain. You are a Timekeeper: one of the select individuals born with a gift that enables you to move and manipulate Time.

We Timekeepers can walk among people of the prehistoric past and just as easily transport to distant futures. The Key of the Nile, which we all possess, marks us from the rest of the population. These powerful keys, descended from Ancient Egypt, represent the hieroglyphic character for eternal life. And in fact, the ability to travel into the past and the future enables us to exist far beyond a human's life span.

Before you proceed, it is crucial to know and understand your gift—a gift that, depending upon how it is used, can lead to either great fortune or terrible tragedy.

—THE HANDBOOK OF THE TIME SOCIETY

## DAY ONE

Walter and Dorothy Windsor lingered over their afternoon tea, peacefully unaware that the one they feared had stolen through the gates to their home. As Walter thumbed through the *New York Times* and Dorothy hummed along to the symphony echoing from the nearby radio, the girl in black strode up the white stone steps and turned the knob of the front door, unseen by the Windsor Mansion's household staff. While her footsteps echoed through the Grand Hall, Walter sweetly reached over to touch his wife's cheek. It had been so long since they'd been happy, and now, with their granddaughter finally in their lives, it seemed they might be getting a second chance.

Suddenly the library doors swung open, and all the light

left the room. Dorothy let out a strangled scream, clutching Walter's hand. Hot tea streamed painfully onto Walter's legs as he knocked over his cup in shock. For a moment the only sound was the frenzied crescendo of the piano and strings from the symphony playing on the radio, until Walter found his voice.

*"Rebecca,"* he gasped.

The door slammed shut and Rebecca Windsor stalked toward them, her mouth curved in a knowing, mirthless smile. Even as Dorothy cowered in her husband's arms, she couldn't tear her eyes away from Rebecca, unable to fathom how a woman long dead could so realistically appear to be herself at age seventeen. She looked just like her chilling portrait from the Windsor family album of 1888, with the same angular pale face, steely dark eyes, and black hair piled onto her head in a fashion that accentuated her sharp, unwelcoming features. The folds of her voluminous Victorian dress swathed around her like drapes of armor. She looked terrifyingly alive, yet there was a translucence to her appearance that made her almost inhuman.

"Why are you here?" Dorothy burst out, her voice thick with tears. "We did everything you asked—you said it would keep her safe, but you lied! Our daughter is dead because of you!" Her whole body shook with agony as she remembered the last time she had seen Rebecca, and the horrors that had followed.

"You failed," Rebecca said coldly. "You *failed* to keep Marion away from Irving, and that is the reason why she is dead, and why we now have Michele on our hands. You were supposed to prevent the girl from being born, not bring her into my house to live!" Her voice rose with fury.

"This hasn't been your house in over a hundred years, Rebecca," Walter shot back. "It's our home now, and we are the only family Michele has. She will live with us for as long as she likes."

"The only family she has? You must be forgetting her father," Rebecca hissed. "Now that you've gone and brought her to New York, it's only a matter of time before she finds him. The girl has inherited Irving's *talent*." She spat out the word.

Walter and Dorothy stared at each other, aghast.

"Yes, that's right. She's gone into the past and made a mess of things. Just as her father sought to destroy my life and took your daughter from you, Michele too is leaving carnage in her wake. Didn't I *tell* you what happens to children born from crossed times?" Rebecca's voice lowered to a deceptively silky tone. "The only remedy is to alter the past. Michele must not exist. It's time for us to work together again."

Dorothy covered her mouth with her hand as if she were going to be sick.

"We won't hurt our granddaughter," Walter snapped.

"It doesn't have to hurt. If you follow my instructions, Michele will simply vanish, as if she'd never been born. What's more, you will have your daughter back." Rebecca's voice lilted as she dangled the carrot before them. "After all, without Irving and Michele, Marion would still be alive today. Wouldn't she?"

"Stop it!" Dorothy sobbed. "Stop torturing us. We trusted you once, and it was a terrible mistake. Why are you *doing* this?"

"That man took everything from me!" Rebecca shouted, her face contorting into a monstrous mask of rage. "I won't stop until there is nothing left of him."

Suddenly, a loud crack sounded in the room. Rebecca reached up in alarm, grabbing at her face, but it was too late. The youthful layers of skin began to peel off, disappearing piece by piece as they fell to the floor, leaving behind a pockmarked skeleton of a face crumpled with wrinkles. Her body shriveled and shrank, a tall teenage frame transforming into that of a grotesque old woman in her last breath of life. Dorothy buried her face into Walter's shoulder, horrified by the sight, but simultaneously feeling a flicker of relief as she remembered from years ago that Rebecca was forced to slink back from where she'd come when her youthful façade faded. Only this time, Rebecca's face betrayed no hint of defeat.

"Seven days," she said, her mouth stretching into a chilling smile. "That's how long I must endure being separated from my physical body—that's how long I'm forced to live like a ghost. It may be painful, but it's hardly any time at all." She leaned forward, a malicious glint in her eyes. "All I have to do is remain in your time for seven days, and then I'll have achieved my full human form and Visibility here in this century. Do you know what that means?" Her now-elderly voice filled with hate. "It means that everyone, not just you two fools, will be able to see me, and when they look upon me they will find a perfect girl of seventeen. It means that I will have human strength once again, combined with my power as a Time-keeper. In seven days, *I can kill Michele myself.* Just like that." Her eyes narrowed. "The choice is yours. Do you want your granddaughter killed—or do you want her to simply disappear, as if she never even existed? You know what needs to be done, and you must decide quickly. As I said . . . seven days is hardly any time at all. I'll be seeing you then."

Rebecca's image wavered above them before disappearing into a spinning wind. Walter and Dorothy clung to each other, their faces stricken.

"What are we going to do?" Dorothy whispered.

Walter didn't answer.

*Michele Windsor dreamt of an antique grand piano in a gilded music room. At first the piano stood alone—but moments later Philip appeared, seated behind the instrument with his fingers resting contentedly on the keys. He began a bluesy ragtime piece, his signet ring catching the light as he played with a passion that could bring chills to even the most callous of people. He seemed to be asking a question as he played, hoping to find the answer in the melody.*

*Michele stepped out of her shadowy corner of the room and caught Philip's eye. His face lit up and he gave her his slow, famil-iar grin, changing the tune to the song he always played for her, Schubert's* Serenade. *Michele sat beside him, and after finishing the song, he raised her hand to his lips.*

*"Didn't I tell you I would find you again?"* he whispered.

Michele smiled and tilted her face toward his, tingling in anticipation of his kiss. In this moment, he was all that existed.

*Philip.*

Michele awoke from the dream, her body still warm from his touch. The sensation of cold linoleum prickled against her skin and she realized with confusion that she had somehow ended up on the floor.

"She's awake!" a familiar voice cried out in relief. It took Michele a couple of moments, but she recognized the voice as belonging to her closest friend in New York, Caissie Hart. She felt strong hands gripping her shoulders and glanced up to see Ben Archer, one of the jock stars of the junior class, pulling her up to a sitting position.

"Michele, can you hear us?" Ben asked urgently.

"Wha—happened?" Michele managed to croak, her throat feeling like sandpaper.

"You passed out," came the deep voice of Mr. Lewis, Michele's history teacher. He stood above her, his face creased with concern. Through her blurred vision, Michele could make out the rest of the class crowding around behind him, all of them eyeing her curiously. She felt her face redden in embarrassment. It was bad enough being the new girl with the famous last name; now she could add "the girl who randomly faints in the middle of class" to her list of attributes. She had a feeling the stares and whispers were going to follow her even more than usual.

"It happened right after the new guy arrived," Caissie whispered in Michele's ear, giving her a funny look.

With a jolt, Michele remembered the boy who had walked into class minutes before. He'd been the spitting image of Philip Walker, bearing the same name and even wearing his ring. *It couldn't have been him*, Michele thought desolately. *I must have imagined that the new guy was Philip.* Still, she felt her heartbeat quicken as she looked up, secretly hoping that Philip Walker might be somewhere among her classmates.

She immediately saw a lone figure standing off to the side. Michele gasped, covering her face with her hands in shock. She peered through her fingers, and he was still there—*Philip*. Time momentarily stood still as Michele's disbelieving mind drank in every detail, from his beautiful piercing blue eyes to the thick dark hair that she had once run her fingers through, the tall and strong body that had held her close, and the lips that sent shivers down her spine with every touch. She hadn't been imagining things—it *was* him! But how could he possibly be here, in Michele's own time?

Weary from fainting, she tried to stand up but found that she could barely raise herself off the floor. Her body seemed frozen, but she could feel a hot current of electricity coursing through her.

"Philip," she murmured, reaching out her hand. A few of the students snickered, while Ben turned to her with a bewildered look; Michele barely noticed. She stared at the resurrected Philip Walker, who inexplicably ignored her outstretched hand, not coming any closer. But he was watching her, his eyes searching.

"I'm going to take Michele to the nurse's office," said Caissie, hoisting her up to her feet. "I think that fall made her loopy."

"I'll help you," Ben offered.

"No," Caissie said a little too quickly. "We'll be fine."

Throughout the exchange Michele was barely present, unable to take her eyes off Philip. She felt an ache from being so close and yet unable to touch him. He was just *standing* there, making no effort to come near her, and Michele felt her first flare of doubt. What if she was imagining things? Could it be a mere coincidence that he looked just like her Philip, that the two of them shared the same name? But then she remembered the signet ring on his finger—and Michele felt certain that Philip Walker had found a way back to her, just as he had once promised.

Michele tried to protest as Caissie led her out of the classroom, but Mr. Lewis insisted. "You're not coming back to class until the nurse confirms that you're all right. I'll be expecting a note from her."

Michele didn't know how she could bring herself to walk away from Philip only minutes after he had inconceivably appeared in her Time. She reluctantly followed Caissie, and as soon as they were in the hall and away from prying eyes, Caissie yanked her into the nearest restroom, her expression rattled.

"*What* just happened in there? I thought you were having a seizure or something! The new guy came in and two seconds later your eyes rolled back and you just . . . fainted." She lowered her voice. "Was it because of his *name*?"

Before answering, Michele quickly threw open each of the bathroom stall doors to make sure she and Caissie were alone.

When she turned back to Caissie, her friend was staring at her as though contemplating whether Michele might have officially gone off the deep end.

"It's not just his name, it's *him*. Philip is back," she said breathlessly.

Caissie sighed. "I was afraid that's what you were thinking. Believe me, I get that it's a weird coincidence for him to have the same name as your Philip, but that's all it could possibly be—a coincidence."

Michele shook her head. "It has to be him, Caissie. He looks *exactly* like Philip, and not only that, he's wearing the same ring that Philip Walker gave me in the 1920s, the one you saw me wearing just last month—the ring that I somehow lost!"

"But Michele, you're the only one who can travel through time. Philip never could," Caissie gently reminded her. "And if the new guy really is your Philip, then why did he just stand there? It didn't seem like he knew you at all."

She swallowed hard. Philip's return was a miracle—she couldn't bear the thought that it might not be real. "Maybe he doesn't want to let on to everyone else that we already know each other? I just need to talk to him. Come on!" With a shot of adrenaline, Michele grabbed Caissie's hand and pulled her out of the bathroom.

"Wait." Caissie stopped her. "Didn't you hear Mr. Lewis? I really do have to take you to the nurse."

Michele hesitated, and Caissie wrapped an arm around her shoulder. "It's okay. He'll still be here when you get back," she said with a slight smile.

It was only when they reached the nurse's office that Michele remembered what she had seen just before fainting: a dark cloaked figure sweeping past the classroom window, seconds after this new Philip's appearance. Though she didn't understand why, the sight had frozen her with terror.

After diagnosing Michele with "exhaustion," the nurse insisted she rest for the remaining hour of class. While any other student would have been thrilled at the invitation to skip U.S. history, Michele could barely sit still with the knowledge that she and Philip were somehow in the same twenty-first-century building. But under the nurse's watchful gaze, Michele had no choice other than to lie on the cot in the sterile starkness of the Berkshire High School infirmary, waiting for the hour to pass. She closed her eyes and the images and sensations of the past two months flooded her mind so vividly, it was as though she were reliving those days all over again. She felt the familiar pang of longing for her mom. There was so much she wished to tell her—if only she could find a way to bend the rules and save her.

It was still impossible for Michele to fathom how life could be forever, irrevocably altered in just twenty seconds. That was how long it had taken for another driver's car to kill her mother, and in those twenty seconds, Michele's former identity as a carefree California girl died with her. Marion Windsor had been more than just a mom—she was Michele's best friend. Though Michele had wished death would come for her too, and bring her back to her mom, it turned out that she was destined to travel even farther.

Marion's will was another devastating blow. Instead of Michele moving in with one of her friends and finishing high school in her hometown, Marion had left clear instructions naming her estranged parents in New York as Michele's next of kin. Less than a month after losing her mother, Michele was forced to move across the country to New York City, enroll in a snooty high school that catered to the offspring of Manhattan's elite, and take her place as the youngest in the Windsor family line—a role she'd thought she would never have to fill.

Marion had hidden from the Windsor name—as legendary in New York as the names Astor, Vanderbilt, and Carnegie— ever since Michele was born. Michele always followed suit in keeping their identity a secret, until the fall afternoon when she moved into the mammoth Windsor Mansion on Fifth Avenue to live with her distant grandparents and an entire household staff. All the while, she wondered what could *possibly* have possessed her mother to send Michele to live with the people whom she herself had escaped.

The only thing she knew was that this great rift centered around her father. Walter and Dorothy Windsor were incensed when their daughter and only heir fell in love with an unknown boy from the Bronx, and they forbade her to marry the lower-class Henry Irving. Unable to face a life without him, Marion ran away with Henry to Los Angeles on the eve of her high school graduation. The Windsors retaliated by offering Henry one million dollars to leave her, and though they claimed he refused their offer, Marion never believed her parents—for he sure enough disappeared, leaving Marion just before she discovered that she was pregnant. For sixteen years, Michele thought that was the whole story of her no-good, absentee father—until New York showed her the truth. Here, she discovered his powerful skeleton key, and learned of his true identity as Irving Henry . . . from the nineteenth century.

When Michele first picked up his key it had *responded,* transforming from an inanimate object into a moving and pulsing talisman, as if it recognized her touch. To her disbelief, the key sent Michele *back in time* one hundred years—and that's where she met the stranger who had haunted her dreams for as long as she could remember. Philip Walker. The man she'd always assumed to be a figment of her idealizing imagination turned out to be an eighteen-year-old boy from 1910.

From the moment she met him at the Windsors' Halloween Ball, he possessed her every thought and emotion with a dizzying intensity. The two of them, both lost in their own times, found the elusive place where they belonged whenever they were together. But the hundred years between them proved too great an obstacle. Their wrenching goodbye was still painfully fresh in Michele's mind, and now that she was away from him, alone in the school infirmary, it suddenly seemed impossible that he could have found a way into the future.

Michele had moved to New York searching for traces of her mother everywhere she looked. Now, ever since her journey to the past, she found herself searching her modern world for the three of them: her father, her mother—and Philip. Could her desperate dreaming have actually manifested one of them into her own Time?

When the bell rang Michele jumped off the cot and, after hastily reassuring the nurse that she was fine, sprinted back to Mr. Lewis's classroom door to catch Philip. She needed to touch him, to know for certain that he was no look-alike, but the living, breathing Philip Walker she loved.

Michele stopped still when at last she spotted him rounding the corner out of the classroom with his back toward her. She took a deep breath, watching as he stopped to check his class schedule. He raked his hand through his hair in a nervous gesture that she remembered well.

"Philip." It came out like a whispered prayer. Though she was a few feet away, he still heard her. Michele held her breath as he slowly turned around, his blue eyes widening when he saw her. But he remained silent, a flush creeping up his cheeks. Her mind raced with confusion. Something was wrong. This wasn't at all the reunion she had imagined. Why wasn't he taking her into his arms, holding her close while giddily recounting how he had made it into the future to be with her? And why did she feel so shy and nervous around him?

"You're *here*," Michele breathed. Her voice sounded different, like it belonged to someone else. "How is it possible?"

Philip gave her a shaky half-smile. "I'm sorry," he said in his familiar low, warm voice. "Have we . . . met?"

Michele stared at him uncomprehendingly. Was this a joke?

But as she waited for the punch line to come, looking hopefully into his eyes, she saw that something was missing from them: recognition.

"Oh, God." She was overcome by a wave of shock, and she backed herself up against the wall. "You don't remember me?"

Philip shook his head slowly. "You must be thinking of someone else." He looked closely at her. "What's your name?"

Michele felt all the air seep out of her. Just before she lost her balance, Philip quickly reached over to help her upright. As his hand closed around her bare arm, she felt a spark of energy, and watched as he drew in a sharp breath.

"You feel it too," she said softly, looking up at him. "You *are* the same Philip, I know it."

Philip let go of her clumsily. "I don't know what you're talking about. I'm—I'm sorry," he stammered. He turned to give her one last questioning look before taking off in the opposite direction, leaving Michele alone, lost for words.

I was a young girl growing up in Virginia when I first saw what I called The Visions. They looked like human beings, yet I knew there was nothing normal about them. Their faces and clothing, the way they styled their hair, all ranged from the thoroughly antiquated to the wildly newfangled. I knew as soon as I laid eyes on them that they weren't from my early-1800s world, and furthermore, no one else could see them but me. I learned to keep quiet about The Visions after hearing my family pronounce me "mad" when I tried to point one of them out. The only person who believed me was my grandmother.

Then the unimaginable happened. After seven days, The Visions solidified. They became real people, men and women who everyone could see, and they adopted the modes and manners of our time. But a series of shocking events always seemed to follow their entrance into our world. Houses burned down from fires with no cause, neighbors went missing, marriages were interrupted, and there was an overall sense of life being thrown off its course. It wasn't until I was in my twenties that I learned the truth of what The Visions were. That was when my grandmother died, leaving me the precious key that she always wore closely around her neck—along with a letter explaining her secret. She was a time traveler. And now, with her key in my possession, so was I.

Grandmother told me that we were just like The Visions—that any time traveler who leaves his or her present lives like a ghost, only seen by Timekeepers and those few humans with the Gift of Sight, until they've been in another time for seven days. The trouble was, Timekeepers weren't meant to stay in a different time long enough to impact it. Even the smallest of actions by an outsider resulted in serious consequences. A well-meaning Timekeeper who attempted to reverse a loved one's death or ill fortune found an even ghastlier outcome. It was clear to my grandmother, and I was equally convinced, that the time traveler's role was only to observe, learn, and protect the natural Timeline. I knew that our power had to be harnessed and focused. This was how the Time Society was born.

By the year of its founding in 1830, I had gathered twenty members across the United States. Decades later, as I pen this Handbook in the year 1880, our Society has grown to two hundred. There are other, older coalitions like ours in Europe and the Middle East; for the most part we all exist as allies.

The Time Society's purpose has always been to find others who possess the Key and the Time-Traveling Gene, so we may use our gifts collectively and become stronger as an entity, preserving the history of America while protecting its future.

—MILLICENT AUGUST,
PRESIDENT & FOUNDER OF THE TIME SOCIETY

Michele stood in the doorway of the Berkshire High School dining room, an airy café filled with white round tables and matching wicker chairs. A long buffet counter snaked through the center of the room, where students lined up to select their dishes. Michele's eyes scanned the buffet line, but there was no Philip Walker in sight.

The rest of the morning passed by in a blur, with Michele barely conscious of her classes. She hadn't seen Philip since he left her outside the U.S. history classroom, but she'd felt his presence all around her. As her English teacher analyzed the hidden messages of Shakespeare's *The Tempest*, Michele was only present in body, her mind dizzily replaying the brief encounter with Philip. And while her math teacher wrote calculus equations on the board, Michele was busy pondering a far more complicated problem: if this twenty-first-century Philip was the same person she'd been with in the past, how could he not know her? And yet if it wasn't the same Philip, then how could he possibly have the very same face, the same body and voice and *ring*?

As she waited in the lunch line her eyes finally found him, seated at a table filled with the beautiful Kaya Morgan and her perky-pretty trio of girls. She couldn't tear her eyes away as Kaya and her friends chattered and giggled in front of Philip, all of them no doubt angling to place dibs on the hottest new guy in Manhattan.

In the short time that Michele had been at Berkshire High, she'd learned that Kaya, a senior, was considered the biggest catch in school. Michele could certainly see why. Kaya was half Japanese and half American, with an exotic beauty that overshadowed the more familiar looks of the other Berkshire girls. She had a body that would let her pass for a Victoria's Secret model, was captain of the girls' track team, and with her mother an acclaimed modern artist from Japan and her father a descendant of the legendary J. Pierpont Morgan himself, Kaya was equally embraced by both New York's aristocratic society and artistic circles. Michele had spoken to her only a couple of times, but she'd liked Kaya right away. She was friendly and smart, not the type to rest on her looks and family name. So Michele watched with a sinking heart as Philip looked at Kaya, captivated. If this was her competition . . . she didn't even want to think about it.

*Still,* Michele reminded herself, *the miracle is that he's here.*

*Even if he somehow doesn't remember me yet—I know he came back for me.*

Philip's eyes met hers across the dining room, and she felt a jump in her stomach. But just as quickly he looked away, like she was nobody. Michele's chest tightened as she slowly headed toward her lunch table.

"Hey," Caissie greeted her when she reached their table. "How are you feeling?"

Michele set down her tray, forcing a smile for Caissie and the third point of their trio, Caissie's best friend and secret crush, Aaron. "I'm fine. What's going on with you?"

"Nothing much, just speculating about the new guy," Caissie replied, giving Michele a meaningful look. "Since Aaron is a total nerd-genius and takes advanced calculus with the seniors, he got to talk to Philip a little." She glanced over at Aaron, who was rolling his eyes at her. "Tell Michele what you found out."

"Okay, but if you two are into him, I have to warn you that he seems kinda tied up."

Michele followed his gaze to the sight of Kaya murmuring something in Philip's ear. She quickly turned her attention back to Aaron and Caissie before the image could implant itself in her memory.

"What did you find out about him?" she asked numbly.

"Not much, only that he's a senior and he just moved into the same apartment building as Kaya Morgan—you know, the fancy-schmancy Osborne building across from Carnegie Hall. His parents got divorced and that's why he moved here with his mom from Hyde Park."

Michele sucked in her breath, digesting the facts. *He's a senior.* So that explained why she hadn't seen him in any of her classes since U.S. history, which was one of the few junior-senior mixed classes offered at Berkshire.

*His parents just got divorced.* She felt a pang of sympathy at the thought of Philip's having to leave his dad and his hometown to start over in a new city—just as she'd had to when her mother died.

*He lives in Kaya's building, the Osborne.* That was why the two of them seemed chummy despite this being his first day at Berkshire. Michele felt an envious knot in her stomach at the thought of them going home to the same apartment building every day. And that name, the Osborne . . . it sounded so familiar.

"Why do I know that place?" Michele wondered aloud.

"It's one of the landmark apartment buildings in the city," Caissie explained, adopting her scholarly tone. As she spoke, Michele thought if anyone was a nerd-genius, it was Caissie and not Aaron. "It opened in 1885 as luxury housing for the rich families of New York, who wanted a 'hotel living' experience, instead of having to keep up big mansions like the one you live in. But later on in the twentieth century, it was better known as the residence of artists and musicians."

Michele sat up straighter. "Really? Like who?"

"Well, Leonard Bernstein actually wrote *West Side Story* there," Caissie told her. "Legend has it that his music room overlooked the Osborne fire escape, and that's how he came up with the idea to set Maria and Tony's classic balcony scene there."

"All right, while you two are having this history lesson, I'm going to get more fries," Aaron announced.

Once he left the table Caissie said under her breath, "Now are you convinced? This new guy isn't your Philip from 1910, he's just a normal dude from upstate New York."

*Not to mention the fact that he* told *me he's not the same person,* Michele added silently. And yet she didn't—*couldn't*—seem to believe it.

Michele slipped into the backseat of the Windsors' black SUV after school, where the family chauffeur, Fritz, was waiting to drive her home. She was still unaccustomed to this ritual of being waited on by household staff. After growing up in a home where money was always scarce, she was torn between pleasure and embarrassment at experiencing the fineries of life. She had the feeling she didn't deserve any of this, that such an over-the-top lifestyle was too much for anyone, and she was constantly reminded that her mother had disavowed this luxurious existence. But Michele had grown especially fond of Fritz and the housekeeper, Annaleigh. It was clear they both cared about her and were anxious for Michele to be happy in this new life.

Fritz drove south from the Upper East Side high school, passing Manhattan's famed museums, distinguished apartment buildings, and opulent hotels, until they reached the white marble Windsor Mansion on Fifth Avenue, standing proudly across from the lush spectacle of Central Park. Michele's eyes still widened every time the car passed through the wrought-iron entrance gates, giving her a full glimpse of the estate in all its glory, from the Corinthian columns to the palazzo design. The Windsor Mansion had been deemed one of America's greatest architectural achievements when it was built in 1887. More than 120 years later, Michele found it no less awe-inspiring.

Following Fritz out of the car, she saw something in the window of the front entrance that halted her steps. A figure dressed in black, surrounded by a foglike veil, was watching her closely. Michele's palms grew clammy, panic bubbling in her chest as she realized this was the same figure she had seen right after Philip appeared in class—just before she fainted.

"What—who—is that?" she stammered, looking at Fritz nervously.

The chauffeur eyed her with confusion. "What are you talking about, miss?"

Michele pointed straight ahead. "That—that person, or *thing,* in the window. Don't you see?"

Fritz glanced at the window and turned back to her with concern. "I don't see anything."

She looked up at Fritz sharply. How could he *not* see the strange being? And suddenly an incredible thought occurred to her, remembering the times when she herself had gone unseen: *Maybe it's a time traveler.*

Michele let out a nervous laugh. "Whoa, that's weird. I—it must have just been a shadow or something."

Fritz frowned, looking closely at her. "Are you sure you're all right?"

She forced her voice to a more casual tone. "I'm fine, honestly. If anything I just need a new contact lens prescription."

As she followed Fritz into the house with trepidation, the veil of fog lifted and the creature at the window became clear. She was a real person—a girl about Michele's age. Her back was still to them as she stared out the window, so all Michele could see was a pile of slithery dark curls atop a tall body dressed in a nineteenth-century black velvet gown.

*So there are other time travelers besides me . . . and my father.* The realization hit Michele with full force and her heartbeat quickened as she thought of Philip. If this stranger in the Windsor Mansion was a time traveler . . . what if Philip was one too? But that wouldn't explain why he didn't know her. Whenever Michele had traveled through time, she always remembered everything.

"Excuse me," Michele said quietly, when Fritz was out of earshot. "Who are—"

But before she even had a chance to finish her sentence, the girl's image flickered and vanished into the air. Michele felt a cold wave of fear wash over her. Somehow she knew that the girl hadn't wanted Michele to see who she was.

*What* was *that? What in the world is going on?* Michele thought frantically. Were her instincts right—the girl was a time traveler—or had Philip Walker's appearance at school turned her into a mental case, complete with hallucinations?

"Michele, hi!"

Her panicky thoughts were interrupted by the middle-aged housekeeper, Annaleigh, striding into the room.

25

"Hey, Annaleigh."

Annaleigh's pale blue eyes peered at her closely. "Are you all right? You look as if you've seen a ghost."

*Maybe I have.*

"Oh—I'm fine." As she spoke, Michele realized that all day she'd been reassuring different people that she was okay. What was *happening* to her? She took a deep breath, unnerved as ever, but determined to at least fake normalcy until it felt real. "How's everything over here?"

"All right, I suppose. I noticed your grandmother having trouble with her breathing this afternoon. She and your grandfather didn't seem to think anything of it, but I encouraged him to take her to the doctor. They just left ten minutes ago."

Michele swallowed hard. "Do you think she's going to be okay?"

"Of course," Annaleigh said soothingly. "I only suggested the doctor visit to make sure."

Michele nodded hopefully. For all the issues she'd had with her grandparents upon moving into Windsor Mansion, she had grown to love them. They were her only family in the world, and though she knew they were getting older, she couldn't imagine ever losing them.

"They instructed me to make sure you stay put until they get back," Annaleigh told her with a wry smile. "They were quite insistent. I hope you don't have plans to go anywhere."

"No plans," Michele told her. "They picked a good day to have me on lockdown." She felt a flicker of worry that her grandparents' request might have something to do with her grandmother's health, but she pushed the thought away, re-

26

minding herself of the many other overprotective moments she'd experienced with Walter and Dorothy since moving in.

Michele clambered up the curving, red-carpeted marble staircase to her room. When she reached the third floor, she briefly leaned over the railing and looked down at the lavish foyer she had just come from, called the Grand Hall. Designed like an indoor open piazza, the Grand Hall was the focal point of the mansion. Marble columns soared up to the gilded, hand-painted ceilings, and plush chaise lounges and armchairs surrounded a large, carved fireplace. Portraits by the masters graced the walls, while a bronze statue and glittering fountain stood beneath the grand staircase. Those who entered the mansion usually drew a gasp at their first sight of the Hall, and even after living there for two months Michele still felt the same sense of awe. Yet she considered her bedroom the most special place in the mansion, having belonged to her mother and a century of Windsor daughters before her.

She'd been shocked by the suite at first, unable to imagine her low-key mom living in this lilac-and-white bedroom fit for a princess, with its delicate eighteenth-century French furnishings, full-size dressing room, marble bathroom, and sitting room large enough to throw a party in. But when she discovered the key from her father and traveled back in time, she met three formidable Windsor daughters from the past who showed Michele that their name stood for something far more important than money or privilege. There was a passion and strength passed down through the Windsor girls, a desire to break past the constraints that bound them, and Michele had watched as they fought for their dreams and used their positions and fortune for good. While she'd grown up ashamed of her secret family identity, she now looked upon the portraits of the bedroom's past inhabitants with a surge of pride.

Closing the bedroom door behind her, Michele opened the top drawer of her white mahogany desk, and pulled out a small box. Though she knew its contents by heart, she still felt a flutter of anticipation upon lifting the lid.

Nestled carefully inside the box were pieces of a man's life. An October 1910 newspaper clipping from the society pages of the *New York Times,* which Michele had scanned from the public library, gave a breathless account of the Windsors' Halloween Ball—the setting where she and Philip had first met. Grainy black-and-white photographs of the ball's most eminent guests were printed alongside the article, and Michele felt her heart constrict whenever she looked at the image of eighteen-year-old Philip Walker. Despite the poor quality, she could still make out his expression. He was looking off into the distance, his gaze intent. There was something beyond the camera that held his full attention, and Michele knew every time she looked at the photo that she was the one he was gazing at.

Underneath the newspaper clipping was Philip's handwritten sheet music for one of the songs he and Michele wrote together in 1910, "Bring The Colors Back." She had written the lyrics and he had composed the music, the two of them falling in love through a composition that expressed to each other what mere words couldn't.

At the bottom of the box were remnants of Philip's later life under the alias of Phoenix Warren, the famous composer and pianist of the mid-twentieth century. A photo from a 1940 back issue of *Life* magazine showed him looking debonair in his middle age, holding up a gold record plaque for his symphony *Michele*—the song that had given Marion Windsor the perfect name for her daughter. Michele still felt goose bumps rise on her neck whenever she thought about it.

The last item in the box was his obituary from December 12, 1992. He had lived a long, fulfilling life, just as he'd promised Michele when they last met. But he had never married, and Michele couldn't shake the feeling that he'd spent the rest of his days looking for her. Had his search finally brought him here? Or was this new Philip Walker just a descendant?

As Michele placed the lid back on the box, she thought there might be one person who had the answers to all this: her father, the very reason she was able to time travel. But Irving Henry was lost in the past, unaware of her existence.

*I can go back in time,* Michele reminded herself. *I can find him.* The thought both thrilled and terrified her. He was the most important person from her past. She would have to be ready.

When the clock struck six, signaling dinner hour at the Windsor Mansion, Michele was still immersed in her online search for any information she could find on the present-day Philip Walker. While most people nowadays had practically their entire lives laid out online for the world to see, Philip was just as elusive on the Internet as he was in person. She couldn't find him on any social-networking sites, and with one of the most common surnames in the country, it took hours to weed through all the search results leading to other Philips. She got up from her desk with a frustrated sigh just as her cell phone beeped with a text message. Caissie's name popped up on the screen.

*What if he's Philip's great-great-nephew or something? That would explain the resemblance, and why the ring was passed down to him,* the message read.

But Philip's family believed he died in the 1920s. *He wouldn't have just shown up and handed the ring to one of them,* Michele thought. There was no explanation—only the undeniable fact that the eyes she'd looked into today were the very same she'd gazed into in 1910.

She slowly made her way to the dining room, lost in her thoughts, but when she stepped in and saw her grandparents, her mind was jerked back to the present. It was clear that something was wrong.

Michele had never before seen her grandparents slouch. Their razor-straight, proud posture was a mark of regal upbringing and seemed to announce their identities whenever they entered a room. But tonight, as Michele stood in the doorway of the marble-pillared dining room, she found Walter and Dorothy wearily hunched over in their seats, Dorothy trembling while Walter murmured something in her ear.

"Is everything okay?" Michele asked, though she was afraid she knew the answer to the question. "What did the doctor say?"

The two of them looked up, both attempting to smooth their expressions into a pretense of calm.

"My health is fine," Dorothy said shakily. "It was nerves. We only went to the doctor to appease Annaleigh. She is very kind, the way she fusses over us."

"What were you nervous about?" Michele asked, taking her seat across from them at the long oak dining table. Before they had a chance to answer, the kitchen maid, Martha, entered, carrying a steaming tureen of soup. That was when Michele saw the photo album resting between her grandparents, and she stifled a gasp.

Since the day she'd moved in with them, Michele had sensed that Walter and Dorothy were hiding something from her. The burden of their secrets shadowed their faces whenever they looked at Michele and stilted all their conversations. She gleaned her first major clue about what they were hiding the night she found this same antique Windsor photo album in the library, opened to a black-and-white snapshot of Irving Henry—depicting him as the family's lawyer circa 1900. Her grandparents' flustered reaction at finding Michele with the photo album confirmed her suspicions that they'd known— and kept hidden—her father's true identity as a time traveler from the past. In recent days, Michele had found herself waiting for the right time to tell her grandparents that she too knew the truth . . . but so far, she hadn't been able to bring herself to speak the words. She was afraid to crack the shell of their secrets, afraid of what they might do when they learned that she was a time traveler too.

Michele gazed at the worn leather cover of the album, engraved with the words *Windsor Family History, 1880–1910*. She had only ever seen the one picture of her father in the book, but it struck her now that there might be more, and she felt her pulse quicken at the thought. As Martha left, her grandfather cleared his throat nervously.

"We have something to tell you."

Michele held her breath as she looked up at them.

"Are you wearing it?" Dorothy asked suddenly, her voice oddly high-pitched.

"W-wearing what?"

"The key!"

Michele stared at her grandmother in incredulous silence.

"She knows you have it—she knows *what you are*—and she'll stop at nothing to destroy you. You're not safe, not so long as you're anything like him—but you can't let the key out of your sight! It might be your only protection."

Chills ran down Michele's spine, and she found she couldn't speak. For a moment the only sounds in the room were the short gasps of Dorothy's panicked breathing.

"I'm not safe from who?" Michele whispered.

Dorothy doubled over in sobs at the question. Michele shrank back at the alarming sight, her heart racing with panic.

"What is it? What's wrong?" she asked frantically.

Walter pushed out of his chair and leaned over Dorothy, rubbing her back. "You're okay, honey. . . . It's going to be okay." He turned back to Michele, his expression tortured. "This has driven your grandmother mad for more than seventeen years. I had hoped it was over, that we would never have to discuss it with you. But I'm afraid we can't keep you in the dark anymore."

*"You're not safe!"* Dorothy wailed.

Frozen in place, Michele watched her refined grandmother lose all composure. The sight was more terrifying than any words could have been.

"Why don't you go up to bed and let me talk to Michele," Walter suggested quietly. "You'll make yourself sick worrying like this. Try to get some rest."

"No." Dorothy took a deep breath. Though she was still trembling, her eyes red, she seemed to regain a bit of control. "I need to be here."

"Please just tell me what's going on," Michele pleaded, her voice strangled. "At this point I can only imagine the worst."

Walter nodded slowly, and Michele braced herself for what was to come.

"About a month ago, you were looking at a photo of Irving Henry in this album," he said. "We told you he was no one important, just the family lawyer in the old days—but we lied. We had to. We thought we were protecting you."

"I knew it," Michele whispered. "You knew who he really was all along, didn't you?"

"How did *you* find out about him?" Walter asked sharply. "We always thought Marion never knew."

"She didn't. It's a long story, but I figured it out when—when I found this," she said, clutching her key necklace. "He'd left it behind for Mom, but she never realized what it was, and she just kept it in her safe at the bank all these years. I found it after she died." Michele lifted the key out from under her shirt. Its reveal had a physical effect on her grandparents. All the color drained from Walter's face, and Dorothy gripped both arms of the chair, struggling to breathe normally.

"Until today, we always wondered and worried that you might be like him. But we never knew for sure," Walter said, his expression a mix of both fear and amazement. "Have you—have you *seen* him?"

"Once," Michele admitted. "For a split second . . . in 1925. But we didn't speak, and I was sent back to my time right away." She almost added that she had also been at her father's funeral in 1944, and had seen her grandfather as a little boy, but she had a feeling that information might send them both over the edge.

Walter closed his eyes, trying to collect himself. He then reached over and opened the photo album to a new page. "This is your father, at the same age he was when we first met him—when he began dating Marion."

Michele leaned over the photograph, hungry for a look at the father she had never known. She felt her heart clench as she gazed at his picture. Irving Henry was the epitome of boyish good looks and charm, grinning in front of a Christmas tree in the Grand Hall. He had wavy hair and a mustache, which made him look even more like the quintessential Victorian gentleman. But Michele was most struck by the similarities she could see between his face and her own, despite the crude quality of the aged photograph, dated Christmas 1887.

"I got my dimples from him," she whispered. "I have his nose. And . . . we have the same smile."

"It caught us off guard when we first saw you," Dorothy said quietly. "Of course you look like your mother . . . but you're so much like him too."

Michele pored over the snapshot, trying to memorize his face.

"Irving was born and raised in this house, with the servants," Walter divulged. "He was the butler's son, and even after his father, Byron, died and he went away to school, he returned to Windsor Mansion on holidays. While it was certainly unusual in those days for the staff to befriend the family they served, the butler was the highest-ranked position in the household, so the Windsors respected Byron. And his son, Irving, grew up with the daughter of the house—Rebecca." Walter turned the page, his expression hardening. "As I heard from the few relatives who knew her back then, she was always a strange girl who no one liked. It seems she and your father, however, were once very close."

Michele peered at the photo Walter was eyeing so grimly and covered her mouth with her hands in disbelief.

The image revealed a girl with dark, soulless eyes, who looked neither young nor old. She was standing in the drawing room of the Windsor Mansion, wearing a long satin dress with a pronounced bustle, her head turned to the side. An upswept pile of black curls framed her sharp face.

Michele staggered away from the album.

"That's her," she choked. "Today—there was a—a ghost of a person following me. I didn't get a clear look at her face, but I know it—*that's her.*"

"She's done it, Walter," Dorothy cried. "She's come after Michele already."

Walter gripped Michele's shoulders. "She can't harm you

for seven days. We know this from the last time she tormented us. She can follow you and frighten you, but she won't have her full physical form and strength until she's been in our time for seven days. That's why we need to get you out of town immediately—"

"Wait." Michele looked from her grandfather to her grandmother, shell-shocked. "How do you *know* all of this? And . . . why? Why would someone from the 1880s want to hurt me?"

She stopped short as her eyes caught the image on the opposite side of the page. She moved in for a closer look and a cold, clammy sensation settled in her stomach. In this snapshot, dated January 1888, Rebecca and Irving were huddled together on the steps of the grand staircase, their smiles secretive.

"This is the last known photo of them together," Walter revealed. "Something happened later that year in 1888, something that caused Rebecca to turn on your father and hate him for the rest of her life—and beyond. To this day, we don't know what it was."

"When Marion brought Irving home to meet us in 1991— he called himself Henry then—we thought he was nothing more than a polite teenager who just wasn't in our daughter's league. We never in our wildest dreams imagined he could be the same Irving Henry I'd known as a boy. We figured it was a harmless young romance and didn't try to stop it. But he and Marion became serious. And that was when Rebecca showed up." Walter's face twisted in anguish at the memory. "Seeing that girl materialize in front of us, decades after her death— there was nothing more terrifying. And yet somehow she gained our trust. She was family, and a powerful time traveler at that. When she proved to us who Irving really was, showed us these very photographs and the secret he had kept from Marion, our first instinct was to believe Rebecca when she said that he would bring about the downfall of our daughter.

"We knew Marion wouldn't believe us if we tried telling her the truth, or maybe we feared that it wouldn't make a difference to her—she loved Irving so much, we were scared that she would follow him anywhere, even to another time. So when Rebecca threatened us into helping her break them apart, we didn't fight her." Walter bowed his head in shame. "I'd been to Irving's *funeral*. I knew he was supposed to have died in 1944—so it wasn't hard to believe Rebecca when she said that he was an abomination, and that his union with our daughter would lead to terrible consequences. She told us that we had to separate them before they could have a child. She was obsessed with that, constantly warning us of what would happen if you were born."

Dorothy spoke up, her voice weak. "We tried to pay Irving to leave Marion. He wouldn't accept the money, but when we finally broke the news that we knew who he was, and that Rebecca had been appearing at our home . . . well, he disappeared the day after that, without a word of warning. But it was all for nothing. Marion never forgave us, and we lost her so early. It was everything we were trying to avoid when we cooperated with Rebecca." Dorothy buried her face in her hands. "And now, after seventeen years, she's come back for you. It's our worst nightmare. But we won't ever listen to that despicable creature again. We know now that she was the real enemy all along."

"You see, Michele, we have always cared deeply for you," Walter said softly. "We kept things from you only because we felt we had no choice."

Michele reached for her grandparents' hands.

"I can't imagine what these years must have been like for you," she said. "It kills me to hear what Rebecca did to you and my parents. But we won't let her win." Michele's teeth clenched with anger as she realized that everything in her life would have been different if it hadn't been for this psychotic time traveler. She would have grown up with both parents and grandparents in her life, Marion wouldn't have been left alone to raise Michele as a single mother—and most of all, Michele wouldn't now be an orphan at sixteen.

"Rebecca broke up my whole family," she whispered as the horror of it all sank in. She looked up at her grandparents. "What does she want to do to me?"

There was an agonizing silence as Walter and Dorothy looked at each other, unsure of what to say.

"She wants me dead, doesn't she?" Michele said flatly.

After a pause Walter said, "But remember, she can't do anything about it just yet. That's why we have to take you away from here. We know you must miss your old home and your friends, so we've booked one-way plane tickets to Los Angeles. We can stay there until the danger has passed."

"No," Michele said firmly. "Rebecca has been terrorizing our family since before I was born—it doesn't matter where I go. She'll find me. That's why I have to be ready when she does. I have to finish this."

"But—but how can you?" Dorothy sputtered. "How can

you stay here when she's haunting the house, and go to school and act normal, when you might only have seven days? At least if we go away—"

"It won't change anything," Michele interrupted. "How do we know she won't just follow us there? The only solution is for me to find a way to stop her—for good." As she spoke, Michele couldn't help marveling at how calm she sounded, despite being thrust into the middle of a real live horror movie. But as she thought of the family Rebecca had stolen from her, fury and determination overrode her fear. Her mind suddenly filled with the image of Philip's face, and the longing to stay alive, to be with him, was so profound that in this moment she felt as if she could defeat any obstacle in her path.

Seizing the album, Michele flipped through it until she found the first visual she had ever seen of her father: his business portrait from the year 1900. He was thirty-one in this photograph, though there was a heaviness to his eyes that made him appear older. The cheerful boy of 1887 was barely visible.

"What I don't understand is, if Irving and Rebecca's friendship ended in 1888, then why was he still working for the family so many years later?" Michele wondered.

"The oddest part is that this photo of Irving was never in the album originally," Dorothy said in a hushed tone. "It appeared the day after he left the 1990s."

"We did some research through the family to find out what we could about Rebecca and Irving," Walter continued. "It wasn't easy, as nearly everyone who knew them had died, but we did speak to her niece, Frances Windsor."

Michele felt a jolt of recognition at the name. She had seen little Frances, known as Frankie back in 1910, when she'd met Clara Windsor. Frankie was Clara's little sister.

"Frances was in her nineties when we visited her in '93, but she still had a sharp memory. Rebecca was her father George's sister, and she remembered her aunt being the strange, unfriendly black sheep of the family. Rebecca never married, nor did she make anything of her life. Frances remembered her always disappearing on mysterious travels, sometimes for years at a time. George inherited this house after their parents died, and Rebecca moved into a townhouse on Washington Square—though she was rarely in the city. According to Frances, her aunt never seemed to want much to do with the family. They only saw her when she made an occasional appearance at Windsor balls. On the other end of the spectrum, as Rebecca drifted away, Irving grew closer to them. Frances said that whenever he came to the house to discuss legal or business matters with her father, he would arrive early and linger after the meeting, as if he was waiting for someone." Walter took a deep breath. "I always wondered if it was Marion he was waiting for—if she was the reason he kept so close."

Michele swallowed the lump in her throat. "Did my . . . my dad ever see Rebecca again?"

"Not that anyone knows of. Rebecca was rarely around, and on the occasions that she did return to Windsor Mansion, Irving must have stayed away. Frances said that although he was invited for holidays and parties at the house, he never once attended."

"I have to find him," Michele declared. "I have this feeling that—that he'll know what to do."

Dorothy gasped, appalled at the idea. "But if you find him, then you could be walking straight into her trap. She lives in his time!"

"Don't worry. I won't do anything until I've figured out more and made a . . . a plan."

Walter squeezed her hand. "We'll help you. We're in this together."

Michele took a deep breath. Seeing the worry written across her grandparents' faces, she wondered if she was deluded in thinking she could take on this cross-century war with an adversary she hadn't even known existed until today. But then . . . she had no choice.

The Key of the Nile is the device that enables us to travel through time. These keys come from the very birthplace of time travel, ancient Egypt. More than two hundred keys are known to exist: one for each family in the Time Society. Though they all form the shape of the ankh, each key has its own unique feature, size, and design.

The Key of the Nile is always given by a Timekeeper within the family before he or she departs this earth. Therefore, time travel is an inherited gift. The power runs in each family's blood, through the Time Travel Gene. The gene is activated when you receive your key.

The vast majority of our kind cannot travel without their Key. Only a select few extraordinary Timekeepers are able.

I am one of them.

—THE HANDBOOK OF THE TIME SOCIETY

When it was time for bed, Michele left her bright desk lamp shining and locked her door, dragging an armchair against it for good measure. She knew logically that none of these precautions could stop a time traveler from entering her room, but it still made her feel a bit safer. Retrieving the newspaper photo of Philip from the 1910 Halloween Ball, she climbed into bed, gazing at it until she finally fell asleep.

*   *   *

"My grandfather's clock
Was too large for the shelf,
So it stood ninety years on the floor. . . ."

Michele stepped forward, toward the sound of a young girl's hushed singing. The tune sounded like a children's nursery rhyme, yet the girl sang it in a sinister tone. Michele felt an odd sense of foreboding as she moved through the grass.

*I'm in Central Park,* she realized as she passed the rippling lake and took in the verdant greenery on either side. *But how did I get here? Where are all the people?*

A drop of water hit her fleece pants, and Michele looked down to see that she was in her sleepwear, with soft slippers in place of shoes. *What in the world?*

A drizzle had begun to fall, and she quickened her pace until she found herself standing in front of an old merry-go-round. The creaky carousel moved in slow motion while droplets of rain hit the colorful carved horses. And then Michele saw them—two children, around eight or nine years old, moving through the mist on the ride. The girl was dressed formally for the park, wearing a white pinafore tied with a yellow sash. The tiny hands holding on to the horse's neck were adorned with kid gloves, and an old-fashioned bonnet framed the girl's jet-black hair. Meanwhile, the little boy was adorably dressed in a petite Norfolk jacket with knee-length trousers.

> *"Ninety years without slumbering,*
> *Tick, tock, tick, tock."*

The sweeter voice of the little boy voice joined the girl's in song.

*"His life seconds numbering,*
*Tick, tock, tick, tock,*
*It stopped short,*
*Never to go again,*
*When the old man died."*

As they finished singing, the little girl suddenly turned her head to face Michele with an expression that made her stumble backward in alarm.

Instead of the innocent look of a child, the girl's pale face was hard and severe, her dark eyes menacing. There was something disconcertingly familiar about her face. Michele knew she had seen it before.

The little girl slid gracefully off the carousel horse and walked toward her, eyes focused on Michele's neck, hands outstretched. Michele reached up protectively, shielding her key necklace.

"What are you doing?" the little boy called out nervously, hopping off his carousel horse.

"Be quiet, Irving." The girl dismissed him.

*It's Irving and Rebecca.*

Michele lost her breath as the little boy turned around to look at her. His face was like a younger male version of hers.

"Dad," she mouthed, but no sound came out. And then the scene turned black.

## DAY TWO

Michele awoke to the music of the Black Keys blaring from her iPod alarm, and at first she couldn't remember where she was.

The strange dream had disoriented her, leaving an unsettled feeling in her stomach. But soon she registered the familiar sight of her bedroom and remembered that it was a school day. She might have a nineteenth-century time traveler to defeat, but first she would be seeing Philip again. The thought was enough to momentarily distract her from Rebecca and her father. Jumping out of bed, she hurried into the bathroom, butterflies dancing in her stomach as she wondered if today would be the day he remembered her—or if it would be the day she discovered who he really was.

But when she reached the bathroom, the sight in the mirror caused her to yelp in alarm. Wisps of grass were stuck to her pants . . . and there were water marks on her T-shirt. She racked her brain, trying to come up with a memory of having gone outside before bed, but she knew she hadn't. It hadn't even rained last night.

The Central Park of her father's youth hadn't been a dream. *She had really been there.* This wasn't the first time she'd traveled against her will, but it was the only time she had mistaken it for a dream.

Michele sank onto the edge of the tub, head in her hands as she tried to make sense of the madness that was fast becoming her new reality. She might have stayed there, frozen in thought, if Annaleigh hadn't buzzed her on the intercom, letting her know Fritz had arrived to take her to school.

Michele hurriedly blow-dried her hair into natural waves and paired her plaid school skirt with a snowy blouse that reminded her a little of the dress she had worn to the Windsor Ball of 1910. She dabbed on concealer to camouflage the dark undereye circles from her lack of sleep, and after a coat of mascara and lip gloss, she felt ready.

Berkshire High, a 110-year-old private school housed in a museumlike building, looked nearly as intimidating as Windsor Mansion. Corinthian columns framed the white stone structure, and the glamorous teenagers of Manhattan's rich and famous leaned against them as they laughed and chattered in the final moments before the morning bell rang. Michele hurried past them, her heartbeat picking up speed as she scanned the crowds for Philip.

When she arrived in U.S. history, she instantly saw him across the classroom. He looked up from his desk as if sensing her, and their eyes locked. Michele clutched the doorframe, his presence still a shock. She could never seem to stop her overpowering, full-body reaction to him, from the lightheaded giddiness to the flip-flopping sensation in her stomach. She knew from experience that the only remedy was for Philip to hold her close, kiss her lips. But as he broke their eye contact and turned back to the textbook on his desk, Michele felt as if she might as well be just a girl with a crush, longing for the boy to notice her. It was such a jarring change from the Philip who had spent his life waiting for her. Michele swallowed hard, lowering her eyes as she made her way to her seat.

At lunch that day, Michele sat at her usual table in the dining room with Caissie and Aaron, but she was silent during most of her friends' banter. Her eyes kept drifting to the table where Philip and Kaya Morgan sat alone, acting even cozier than the day before. She couldn't hear their conversation, but could see Kaya talking animatedly while Philip nodded and smiled.

"You would think the new guy has superpowers, the way the girls here are freaking out over him," Aaron said unhelpfully as he followed Michele's gaze. "You too?"

Michele didn't see much of a point in lying to Aaron. "There is something about him," she admitted.

"What about Ben? Aren't you going to the dance with him?" Aaron asked.

Michele winced. In all the craziness from the past two days, she had completely forgotten about agreeing to be Ben Archer's date to the school's annual Autumn Ball—which was this Saturday. Ben had seemed cool with going just as friends, but he'd made his crush on her clear. She couldn't imagine dancing with Ben all night while Philip was in the same room. As if reading her mind, Caissie shot her a look.

"You're *not* turning Ben down now," she said, her voice stern even through a mouthful of salad.

"I would never do that!" Michele said indignantly. "I just—"

But she didn't finish her sentence, because at that moment Kaya let out a flirtatious laugh, squeezing Philip's hand as he grinned at her.

"Never mind. I'm lucky to be going with Ben." Michele took a deep breath. *It's going to be okay. He's only acting so close with her because she's the one person he knows at this school.* She refocused on her friends, casting around for a change of subject. "Are you guys going to be here for Thanksgiving?"

As Caissie and Aaron commiserated over splitting the holidays between their divorced parents, Michele subtly scooted her chair around so she'd have less of a view of Philip and Kaya. For a good ten minutes she managed to keep herself from looking at him, until they stood up to leave. That was when Michele saw the veiled figure materialize through a fog in the middle of the dining room—*Rebecca*. Her image flickered like that of a ghost, but Michele could see her watching Philip closely. *What could Rebecca want with him?*

"Um, Michele. What are you doing?"

Dazedly, Michele glanced over at her friends, who were eyeing her in bewilderment. She realized she had stood up at the sight of Rebecca—and it must have looked to Caissie and Aaron like she'd gotten up to blatantly stare at Philip and Kaya.

"I, uh, thought I saw someone from California," Michele fibbed, blushing as she sat back down. She breathed a sigh of relief as the dark fog of Rebecca evaporated just as quickly as it had appeared. Philip was safe . . . for now. Michele would have to make sure he stayed that way.

Michele dialed the Windsor Mansion from her cell as Fritz drove her across Midtown after school. She heard Annaleigh answer as the SUV passed the busy lights and bustle of the West Fifties.

"Hey, Annaleigh. I just wanted to give you the heads-up that I'm on my way to, um . . . study with a friend. Fritz is driving me. I'll be home for dinner, but I just thought my grandparents would want to know." Michele silently prayed that Walter and Dorothy wouldn't have a panic attack over her going out after school when Rebecca was at large—but then, Michele knew she wasn't any safer at home. If anything, she needed to get as much accomplished as she could during the next six days, before Rebecca became far more threatening.

Fritz dropped her off at the corner of Fifty-Seventh Street and Seventh Avenue, across from the stately Carnegie Hall, but she only had eyes for the building farther down the block, the Osborne. The apartment's brownstone exterior seemed to beckon her, and a sudden breeze felt like a whisper urging her forward. She didn't have any sort of plan, and she knew that showing up at his apartment could give off a total stalker vibe. Still, she had to talk to him, away from the distractions of school. She needed to find out why he couldn't remember her, who he really was—and why Rebecca might be following him too.

Her heart thudded in her chest as she approached the building and noticed the plaque above the front door: *Established 1885. A New York City Designated Landmark.* Street-level storefronts surrounded the Osborne, with a break in the center for its main entrance. She peeked into the window of the lobby, and drew in her breath.

It looked as if the interior of a Renaissance palace had been transplanted into this Manhattan apartment building. The Osborne lobby was an artistic masterpiece, its walls and floors completely covered in decorative marble and mosaics. The curved and coffered ceilings were just as ornate, while the entrance was flanked by painted medallions illustrating the subjects of music and literature. Antique wall sconces shined a spotlight on the focal point of the lobby: a gold-and-bronze antique Roman clock, sitting proudly on a heavy pillar at the back of the room. Michele stared at the clock, and without thinking, slowly reached for her key.

The breeze in the air escalated into a high wind swirling around her body, and Michele gasped as her feet were lifted off the ground. Spinning so fast that she could hardly see, she realized with amazement that *it was happening again.* She landed with a stumble in front of the Osborne at dusk—but everything else had changed.

The first thing she noticed was the noise. The city sounded altogether different. She heard the *chug-chug* of a train, the rumble of old-fashioned cars, and the musical quality of voices speaking in refined tones, as if they were acting in a play. Michele turned around slowly, her eyes growing wide.

Barreling down the streets were opulent cars that couldn't have looked more different from the twenty-first-century models Michele was used to, from a turquoise, white-roofed Cadillac to a brown open Buick that resembled a stagecoach. The men driving were dressed in wide-lapelled suits, patterned neckties, and brimmed hats, while the women seated beside them wore puffed-sleeve blouses with small asymmetrical hats, their hair styled in short, blunt curls framing their faces. An antique yellow bus zoomed past, bearing a movie poster. *Cecil B. DeMille's* Cleopatra, *starring Claudette Colbert! Don't miss the cinematic masterpiece of 1934!* Overhead, the elevated railroad rattled and puffed along tracks above Seventh Avenue.

*It's 1934,* Michele thought in awe. *I'm in 1934!*

A new sound now overrode the others—a piano, coming from one of the second-story front windows of the Osborne. The musician was playing with a passion and skill that Michele had heard from only one other person in her life. The piece was one she knew well: *Serenade.*

Michele stared up at the window, her whole body trembling. *Is it really him?* And then she saw the outline of his face through the windowpane, his eyes closed in concentration as he played, tendrils of dark hair falling over his forehead.

"PHILIP!" Michele cried. He shouldn't have been able to hear her, not when her voice was nearly drowned out by a truck's blaring horn. But he turned, his face frozen, as if doubting what he had heard. Then he saw her, jumping up and down on the sidewalk across the street, and his face broke into an astonished smile. She found herself running to him, scaling the fire escape to his window. *Just like Tony and Maria,* she thought with a joyful laugh.

Philip threw open the window and climbed out, his eyes welling with tears as he looked at her. For a moment he just stared, blinking rapidly as if trying to prove to himself that what he was seeing was real—that Michele was back. As she gazed at him, Michele felt the same nostalgic ache in her stomach that she remembered from the only other time she had seen him all grown-up, in 1944—the last time they saw each other. But he would have no idea about that meeting now. It was in his future.

"Michele," he whispered.

In an instant she was in his arms. She nestled her head against his shoulder, breathing in his familiar scent that was like a balm to her frayed nerves. But Philip gently pulled away from their embrace, his expression heartbroken.

"I wish you had come back sooner," he said quietly. "I grew up."

"I know. If I had any control over this, I never would have left 1910. I would have stayed with you the whole time." Michele shakily sat down on the top step of the fire escape and Philip joined her. As they looked at each other, Michele thought that his face was almost the same as when he was a

54

teenager, but there were lines around his eyes now. Although nearing middle age, he was as handsome as before, looking like a classic matinee idol in his drape suit.

"All these years have gone by since I saw you last and now here you are just the same." Philip's voice broke. "Where have you been keeping yourself all this time? What have your days held? Have you been happy? I want to know everything. You're the question that has haunted me, that I've wondered about every day since I was eighteen."

Michele reached for his hand. "I wish I had the right answers. What's been an eternity for you has been no time at all for me. I'm just the same girl you knew in 1910, no different. You're the one who has grown and changed. I want to know everything about you. Are you . . . are you happy?"

Philip gave her a tremulous smile. "Well, I've kept my promise. I've done well with my music, thanks to you. I'm motivated by wanting you to have something left of me in our world."

Michele blinked back the tears. "I'm so proud of you—of everything you've become. And . . . you kept your other promise, didn't you? You found a way back to me. Only you don't seem to remember."

Philip sat up straighter, letting go of her hand. "What do you mean?"

For a moment Michele wondered if she shouldn't have said anything, if she might change the present by telling him about it in the past, but it was too late. She had to know for certain if he and the new Philip were one and the same, and why he didn't remember her.

"Yesterday you showed up in my time—at my school,"

Michele revealed, watching as Philip's jaw dropped. "You looked the same as you did when we first met, when you were eighteen. You were even wearing the same signet ring. But for some reason, you didn't remember me. And again today, you were spending time with another girl and looking at me like I was just another one of your classmates, no one special." The tears Michele had been holding back trickled down her cheeks. "How is any of this possible?"

Philip gripped his chest, staring at her in shock. "I—I don't understand. You're saying that my younger self went into the future? How could that happen without me remembering it?"

"It all sounds so crazy, I know. But he has your face, your voice, your ring; he even lives in this building! *Everything* about him is just like you . . . except for the way he is with me." Michele wiped her eyes.

Philip was silent for a moment, and when he spoke again his voice was filled with wonder. "When I was younger, after you first left, I would while away days just dreaming of another life with you. I'd imagine that I was another person, born in your time, and that we could be together in every sense of the word. Do you think—could I have actually made that *happen*?"

"I wish there was a way we could find out." An idea occurred to her. "Do you have anything . . . anything I can give to the new Philip, like a clue? Something to help him remember?"

Philip thought for a long moment. "I'll be right back." Climbing in through the window, he gathered some papers off his grand piano and returned to her on the fire escape. "This is the song I was working on when I saw you outside. I only have a chorus and a bridge, no verse yet. Give this sheet music to him, and then the two of you can finish it. This is the way to remind him of us, and of who he used to be." He gave her an emotional smile. "After all, writing music together is how we fell in love."

Michele felt her heart constrict at his words. She took the sheet music, holding it close to her. "What if this new you isn't a musician?"

He grinned, and for a moment Michele could see the teenager in him again. "He will be. There's no way any version of me can exist without my music."

Michele smiled back at him. But there was something more she needed to say, and her expression turned serious.

"Philip, I need you to do something for me. Please— whatever you do, stay away from Rebecca Windsor."

His eyebrows rose. "Violet's aunt?" he asked in bemusement. "I haven't seen her in ages. Why?"

Michele hesitated.

"You can tell me."

She took a shaky breath. "There's no easy way to say this. Rebecca can time travel too, and—she wants me dead. She's come into the future, into my time. And today I saw her, like a ghost, watching the new Philip Walker in a way that made me think she has something against you too. So please, don't give her the chance to want to hurt him—*you*. Whatever you do, stay away from her."

Philip's face was ashen.

"*Why?* Why does she want to hurt you?"

"That's what I'm trying to figure out. I only know that it has something to do with my father."

Philip swallowed hard, and when he looked at her his face

was filled with despair. "I can't stand being helpless—knowing you're in danger and there's nothing I can do, that I'm dead in the ground in your time, unable to do anything to protect you."

At that moment Michele felt Time begin its pull on her body. Her stomach lurched, longing for just another few moments with him.

"You *are* helping me. Just by staying away from Rebecca, you could be helping me more than we both know. I'm being sent back to my time, but—I love you, Philip. At any age, in any body, in any era . . . I love you."

"I love you!" Philip called, watching as the wind lifted her off the fire escape. "I will do anything I can from here in the past to keep you safe."

Moments later, she found herself back on the twenty-first-century sidewalk in front of the Osborne, surrounded by familiar modern smells and sights. Her eyes remained on the second-story front window, which was now empty. And then a figure drifted by, that of the present teenage Philip Walker.

Michele was just about to race into the lobby and up the stairs to show him the sheet music, when she saw another person beside him: Kaya Morgan, looking up from a textbook and laughing at something he'd just said. So their relationship had progressed to study dates. That was fast.

Michele backed away from the Osborne, heading toward home. Though it stung to see Philip with Kaya, she didn't feel defeated—she couldn't, not with the pages in her arms, and the incredible discovery that Philip had returned not only to her, but to the very same apartment where he had lived decades in the past.

The Gift of Sight is the ability for ordinary human beings, those with no powers, to see and interact with spirits and time travelers. Sometimes known as mediums, many of the people who possess the Gift believe they are seeing ghosts. In actuality, the apparitions they see are not ghosts, but time travelers who have not yet reached Visibility or their full physical form in the alternate time.

We have found that the Gift of Sight runs in families. As of this entry in 1880, our experiments show that five percent of families in the United States carry the Gift. This means we Timekeepers must always be on alert. Our actions in the past and future can be seen.

—THE HANDBOOK OF THE TIME SOCIETY

## DAY THREE

Michele arrived at Berkshire High on Friday morning to find Caissie waiting for her by the columns at the front entrance. As soon as Michele caught up with her, they both said, "I have something to tell you."

"You go first." Michele noticed her friend's awkward expression. "Are you okay?"

"I'm fine. It's just—well, you know how I made the unfortunate decision to add Kaya Morgan as a friend on Facebook?" Caissie rolled her eyes sheepishly. "Well, I wanted you to hear it from me, and not through the school grapevine. One of Kaya's groupies wrote on her wall that she and Philip Walker are going to be the hottest couple at the dance. He's taking her to the Autumn Ball."

Michele shut her eyes, flashing back to the previous night when she had watched Philip in 1934 playing their song. *He wouldn't go out with another girl, not now that he's found me again. He wouldn't.*

"I know, it sucks," Caissie continued. "But . . . I think it's proof that he really isn't your Philip. Because from everything you've told me, the Philip you knew only ever wanted to be with *you*. He would never come into the future only to waste time dating another girl. It makes no sense."

"I get what you're saying," Michele said quietly. "But— something happened. I went to the Osborne after school yesterday." She gave Caissie an embarrassed smile. "I know, you're probably thinking I've turned into a stalker. But I just *needed* to talk to him. I was wearing the key, and it sent me back in time to 1934. And he was there, Caissie. I saw him in the window. He was playing piano, playing our song. The two Philips not only look the same, but they share the same ring, and now he's living in the same apartment that my Philip spent his later life in. How can they *not* be the same person?"

Caissie stared at her in amazement.

"He gave me something to give Philip—a song that he thinks could be a clue to help him remember," Michele confided. "I have to find the right time to give it to him."

"This is just . . . crazy," Caissie declared. "So your Philip really thinks the new Philip is *him*?"

"Well, he was shocked by what I told him, so he obviously had no memory of traveling to the future when he was younger.

But he did think it had to be him—or some version of himself. I mean, how else do you explain the resemblance and the ring and all of it?"

Caissie shook her head. "For the first time in my life, I have no answer."

The bell rang and the two girls hurried inside. Michele noticed something new decorating the walls: posters advertising the theme and location of the Autumn Ball. She'd learned from Caissie that the Berkshire tradition was for the planning committee to keep these details secret until the last minute, which usually resulted in a mass exodus to the shops on Fifth Avenue the day before the dance.

*Dress in your finest threads for a true Gilded Age Autumn Ball!* The words seemed to leap off the poster as Michele glanced at it. An illustration of a gown-clad Gibson Girl dancing with a dapper-suited gentleman filled the center, while underneath was emblazoned: *The Empire Room at the Waldorf-Astoria Hotel. November 19, 8 p.m.*

Michele couldn't help chuckling as she looked at the poster. The theme was too ironic. They might as well have been promoting the 1910 Halloween Ball where she had first met Philip.

"I have to say, our school is probably the only one pretentious enough to go with Old Money as the theme," she heard a male voice say jokingly behind her.

Michele turned around to see a grinning Ben Archer.

"Yeah, it's not going to be a rager," she agreed. "Hopefully you know how to waltz. If this really is an old-school ball, I can tell you on good authority that there won't be much rock or hip-hop."

"Don't worry. I always impress on the dance floor," Ben said with a wink.

But Michele's smile froze on her face when she saw Kaya and Philip swing through the doors together into the hallway.

"Come on, you guys. We should get to class," said Caissie, following her gaze.

Ben fell into step with them and they had no choice but to face Philip and Kaya, who were approaching the same classroom from the opposite end of the hall. Philip met Michele's eyes, and Ben chose that moment to snake his arm around her shoulder. Philip looked away, but not before furrowing his brow at the sight of Ben's arm around her.

*What if I'm the only one who ever remembers?*

For the third straight lunch in a row, Michele had the misfortune of watching the Philip & Kaya Show. It was enough to dull all other emotions, even her fear of Rebecca and the battle that she knew lay ahead of her.

*What if it's just me who feels the missing touch, hears the sound of laughter long gone, and sees the two of us in a forgotten New York?*

Philip seemed to look through Michele, his expression unfazed and innocent, and it was that ambivalence that seemed to mock her. *Could he be playing a role . . . or did he actually forget me?*

She couldn't look away. Philip's blue eyes sparkled as he and Kaya shared a joke. He broke into his signature smile, and for the first time, Michele found it heartbreaking. *But then, isn't that always the case with a smile—when you know it's not meant for you?*

She wished she could stop this speeding train of jealousy, but she couldn't help it. To have him back, just as he'd promised, but not remember what they once had? It was as though Time was playing a particularly cruel trick.

And then his glance met hers. She'd been caught staring, but she held her gaze. So did Philip. She noticed Kaya touching his arm, trying to regain his focus, but he looked at Michele a moment longer than he should have before turning back to his lunch date.

It was a small victory, but she savored it. He couldn't have forgotten her completely.

As Michele walked to study hall that afternoon, she was stopped by a lilting melody echoing off the school walls. The piano keys sounded like they were flying, dancing, and then wailing in a breathtaking blur of music. Michele knew of just one person who could play like that.

She turned around, breaking into a run as she followed the noise through the hallway. As the piano playing grew more frenzied, she reached the door to a room she hadn't seen before. Gingerly stepping inside, she found herself in some sort of choir room, filled with music stands and band equipment. In the corner of the room, his hands moving majestically over the piano while his body swayed to the rhythm, was Philip.

Michele's eyes closed. For a moment she was transported back to 1910, to the candlelit nights in the Walkers' music salon, sitting beside Philip as he played his newest compositions just for her. When she blinked her eyes open, she almost expected to find herself inside the extravagant Walker Mansion instead of the casual school choir room. The sight of Philip in the Berkshire uniform of khaki pants and navy blue polo shirt, instead of his black suit and white tie, jarred her senses. The only thing that hadn't changed was his playing, which sounded as incredible as when she first heard it—as beautiful as it had been last night, in 1934.

Philip glanced up. Upon seeing Michele his hands froze, cutting the song off abruptly.

"I didn't see you there."

"I'm sorry. I didn't mean to interrupt. I heard the piano and . . . I just had to see who was playing."

Philip couldn't help smiling, and Michele's breath caught in her throat. It was the first real smile he had given her since arriving at Berkshire, and it gave her the confidence to take a step closer to the piano.

"The way you play—it reminds me of someone," she began.

Philip looked away. "Not that same guy you thought I was the other day?"

Michele let out a nervous chuckle. "You sound just like the pianist Phoenix Warren."

Philip studied the keys. "Funny—my piano teacher says the same thing."

*Now—now is the time to show him the sheet music,* Michele thought. But something held her back. She felt a disconcerting distance between them, as though they had only just met, and she wondered if the clue might go over better after having a real conversation.

"What were you playing?" she asked. "I loved it."

"You did?" Philip looked pleased. "I wrote it."

Michele stifled a gasp. *Philip was right.* There would never be a version of him in any Time that wasn't a musician. If she'd had the slightest doubt that the two were one and the same, she was now more convinced of their connection than ever.

"What kind of music do you write?" Michele made a valiant effort to keep her voice steady.

"Everything. Classical and jazz are my favorites to play, but I write a lot of pop and rock."

"Do you perform your own stuff?"

Philip laughed. "Nah, I'm not the greatest singer. I write for other artists."

Michele watched him in fascination. She could tell by his ease that this new Philip had more confidence about his music than the eighteen-year-old she had known in 1910. It was as though the twenty-first century had given him a new fortitude.

"Who were you writing that song for?"

"Ashley Nichol," Philip replied. Michele's eyebrows shot up at the name of the twenty-year-old Grammy winner. "I've sold two other songs to her, but she hasn't done anything with them yet."

"Third time's got to be the charm, then." Michele smiled. "That's really amazing, though, to be selling songs to a major artist when you're still in high school! How did you do it?"

"Thanks. Well, I've been writing and playing forever, and one night two years ago I got a gig opening for a singer/

songwriter friend at Joe's Pub. This was obviously before I realized I wasn't cut out to be a singer." He grinned. "But a music publisher happened to be in the audience that night, and she liked my songs and signed me to a deal. Since then, I've been recording demos after school and on the weekends, and she pitches them to artists. It's been really cool," he said modestly.

"I'll say." Michele took a deep breath before asking the question. "Do you write everything yourself? Music and lyrics?"

"Yeah, but I'm a lot better at the music," Philip admitted. "My publisher keeps trying to set me up with different lyricists, but I haven't really felt it with any of them."

Michele's mouth fell open. Philip's words from last night in 1934 echoed in her ears. *This is the way to remind him of us, and of who he used to be. After all, writing music together is how we fell in love.* It felt as though he had somehow orchestrated all of this from the past, providing her with an opening back into his life.

"How about giving me an audition?" she asked lightly. Philip's expression turned wary, and Michele quickly added, "No pressure. It's just that I've been writing lyrics for as long as I can remember, and I have the opposite problem you do—I'm way more skilled with words than music."

Philip gave her an amused smile. "Okay, why not. I'll just keep playing the song and I guess we'll see what you come up with."

As he played the tender melody, a title came to Michele immediately. "I Remember." She pulled a notebook and pen out of her school bag, and soon the words were pouring onto the page.

> *You've got a new life now,*
> *You're free from old ties.*
> *I can't understand how,*
> *Was all I knew a lie?*
> *We could live all we ever dreamed*
> *If you'd just remember you love me*
> *'Cause I . . .*

And then the chorus flew from her pen in a simple, urgent plea.

> *I remember*
> *The way you used to hold me.*
> *I remember*
> *The thrill we used to share.*
> *We seem to be*
> *Strangers passing by now.*
> *Tell me, did you forget how*
> *We once cared?*

She looked over what she'd written, a self-conscious flush heating up her cheeks. She hadn't meant to write something so personal . . . and the lyrics were far simpler than what she usually wrote. For a moment she hesitated, but then she gathered her resolve. She knew her words would fit the song.

"I have a verse and chorus," Michele called to him over the sound of the piano. "Want to hear it and let me know if I'm on the right track?"

Philip looked at her in surprise. "That was fast. Yeah, let's hear it."

She moved toward him, her heart thumping loudly in her chest.

"I'm not much of a singer either, but here goes." Michele began to sing to Philip's melody, looking down at the piano keys shyly. She started off shaky but gained confidence as she reached the chorus, and dared to glance up at him as she sang:

*"I remember*
*The way you used to hold me.*
*I remember*
*The thrill we used to share . . ."*

Philip looked away, but Michele could see that his body had become still. When she finished the song he glanced at her in a way that showed she had moved him.

"That was great," he said softly. "It's not what I would have done, but I like it. It fits the song."

Michele felt her body warm with pleasure. "I'm glad you think so. Should we try it again with the piano?"

Philip nodded. As she sat beside him on the piano bench, she felt her senses heighten. They were close enough to touch—close enough that with just a turn of the head, his lips could meet hers.

Philip leaned over to arrange his sheet music, his hand

70

brushing against Michele's in the process. He quickly moved it, but she saw that he was breathing faster than normal, his eyes filled with an expression she hadn't seen in a long time.

He began to play, and as Michele sang along quietly, her words were a seamless blend with his music. She studied him, his forehead creased in concentration, and for a moment she once again felt transported to the previous century, seated beside the Philip who would look at her with desire, who always had just the right melody for her words.

*It is you,* she thought with amazement. *I know it's you.* And suddenly, it felt like the right time.

"What's wrong?" Philip glanced at her. "You stopped singing."

"Yeah, I . . . I need to tell you something."

Philip's hands moved away from the piano keys. "Okay."

"Remember when I thought you were someone else, someone who was also named Philip Walker?"

Philip cracked a smile. "How could I forget a weird moment like that?"

"I feel more sure now than ever." Michele's words tumbled out in a rush. "I hate to sound crazy, I know you don't remember so I must seem like a nut job to you but I swear I'm not, and I need you to know . . ." She took a deep breath. "The Philip I knew was a musician too. He asked me to give you this, to help you remember." She reached into her bag and pulled out the music.

Philip hesitated, his expression confirming that he *did* think she might be a nut job, but still he took the pages. He glanced over the sheet music and did a double take, his eyes

71

widening with shock. The piano bench scratched against the floor as he jumped up.

"How did you do this?" he demanded, shaking the papers in front of her. *"How?"*

Michele swallowed hard. She had never seen Philip angry. "I—I don't know what you mean."

"How did you do it?" he repeated as all the color drained from his face. "How did you copy my handwriting—and *read my mind*?"

His panic was starting to rub off on Michele. What in the world had 1934 Philip written?

"I honestly don't know what you're talking about," she pleaded. "I don't read music. What are you seeing?"

Philip stared from her to the sheet music and back again. "It's the song we were just working on. But—I never played you the bridge. I hadn't worked it out yet, it was only in my mind. How did you *know* it?" He backed toward the door but didn't walk through, seeming to struggle to decide whether to get away from her or hear what she had to say.

Michele's jaw dropped as Philip's words hit home.

"I—I had no idea. This is incredible." She took a tentative step closer to him. "Please—I know it sounds too unbeliev-able to be true, but try to hear me. There's *someone you used to be.* No two people can write the same exact song—you and the Philip Walker I knew are the same. He told me this music would remind you—"

Michele stopped short at a loud snap. She glanced up as the overhead lights suddenly flickered and the room turned black. It was far darker than it should have been for the afternoon, even with the lights out, and the chill running down her spine told her that something was very wrong.

"What the—?" Philip threw open the door, but the darkness pervaded the halls. Suddenly, with a strangled yell, he hurtled back into the choir room, throwing himself in front of Michele. For a moment she was too distracted by his closeness to see what he was looking at, but then her eyes caught a tall cloud of smoke winding its way into the choir room, coming straight toward them. Michele was too frightened to move a muscle as it drew closer, coils of black hair and billowing skirts gleaming through the smoke. *Rebecca.*

"Get away from us!" Philip growled, reaching back to grasp Michele and hold her steady behind him. *What made Philip go from not remembering me to suddenly protecting me?* she thought, staring at him in bewilderment. And more importantly . . . why wasn't Rebecca's presence a shock to him? He was no doubt horrified by the sight of her, but something in his voice alerted Michele that he had seen her before.

She and Philip were so focused on Rebecca's terrifying tower of smoke that they didn't hear the footsteps behind them. Suddenly Michele yelped as she felt a hand pulling at her necklace, catching her off guard. She grabbed frantically at her neck, feeling nothing but bare skin. The key was gone.

*"No!"* she screamed, struggling to break out of Philip's grasp and follow the footsteps she heard clattering out of the darkened room. Rebecca slithered away in her cloud, a sense of victory following her out the door.

"What are you thinking, trying to go after her?" Philip said sharply.

"She took my key! It's gone!" Michele's body was racked with sobs as terror seized her. It was one thing to be strong in the face of Rebecca's threat when she had the key, when she had the power to time travel her way out of danger. But now she was completely on her own—exposed and defenseless.

"She didn't touch you," Philip said gently, turning around to face Michele. "I was watching her the whole time."

"Who else would have taken it?" Michele whispered.

At that moment, a crackling noise echoed throughout the room as the lights flickered back on. Philip awkwardly let go of her, his face a mix of emotions.

"Students, we've just experienced a power outage," came a crisp voice over the school PA system. "All of you in the halls, please return to class at once. Everything is back in order."

"I have to get out of here. Are you going to be okay?" Philip asked in a low voice.

"Please just tell me—how come you can see her too?" Michele blurted out.

Philip raked his hand through his hair, his expression desperate as he stammered, "I—I can't talk anymore—I have to go. This is too much—too much." And after one last look, he flew out the door.

She watched him go, her mind returning to what he had said moments earlier—that Rebecca hadn't taken the key. Was there any possible hope that, in her heightened state of fear, Michele might have imagined someone ripping the key off her neck? Could it have simply been the case of a loose chain falling off and lying somewhere on the floor? Deep down, Michele knew it was unlikely—but she had to check. Getting onto her hands and knees, she searched the floor and rummaged under the piano and chairs. But there was still no sign of the key, or the chain that had held it.

Michele stood frozen in the middle of the choir room, her stomach churning. The key was *everything*. Besides being her only possible defense against Rebecca, it was her sole method of traveling through time. The key was her only connection to her father and it was the power that had brought her to Philip. What would she do without it?

*T*he Time Society offers a number of positions for members who seek careers within our world. One of the most important is that of the Detectors, whose purpose is to locate unregistered time travelers. It is a crucial task, for the time travelers who remain hidden are generally those who stay in the past or the future long enough to effect change—and cause considerable damage along the way. By seeking out undiscovered time travelers and introducing them to our Society, we gain valuable members who help us protect the natural Timeline. They in turn receive a wealth of knowledge, power, and membership to a Society that most can only dream of.

—THE HANDBOOK OF THE TIME SOCIETY

Michele headed straight for her room after the disastrous day at school, still in a stupor over the loss of the key. Her mind spun as it replayed Rebecca's terrifying appearance and the moments of hope and confusion with Philip; there was so much that she couldn't seem to make sense of. She ached with the longing to return to twentieth-century Philip, to confide in him and hear his answers. The thought of never being able to find him again was too much to bear, and Michele had to force it away, along with the dread rising in her stomach.

She curled up on the couch in her sitting room, glancing up at the portraits lining the walls. The subjects of each framed painting were different Windsor heiresses of the past, each painted on the occasion of the girl's debut into society at age sixteen, from Clara Windsor in 1910 to Marion in 1991.

Thankfully there was no portrait of Rebecca. Michele wondered if her grandparents had it removed.

Michele was always comforted by the painting of her mother, by seeing her smile shine and her eyes sparkle through the canvas. Marion's far-off voice echoed in Michele's memory: *"Count your blessings, not your worries."*

"If only you were still here," she whispered to her mother's portrait. Michele felt a pang of grief thinking about the plan she had come up with the night before to defeat Rebecca. The first step had been to find out every detail of her and Irving's relationship so she could discover Rebecca's true motive. The final step would have been traveling back to the moment she and Irving became enemies, changing the past to end her vengeance before it began. The thought of what she might have returned home to if the plan succeeded filled her with such regret, it stung to even think about it. If she could have managed to block Rebecca's treacherous path before it reached her parents, then she might have had a father and mother—together and *alive*. But now, without the key . . . it was too late.

A knock sounded at the door.

"Come in," Michele called listlessly.

Her grandparents stepped into the room, Walter carrying a bulky black camcorder that looked like something out of an eighties movie.

"Hi," she greeted them, fixing a smile on her face. She'd already decided against telling them about the stolen key. Knowing Dorothy's mental state was dangling by a thread, she feared this information would send her over the edge. Michele also suspected that if her grandparents knew she no longer had the key's power and protection, they would likely ship her off to hide out as far from Manhattan as possible. Bleak as things looked, Michele *couldn't* leave New York. She couldn't go anywhere as long as Rebecca was still after her family. She owed it to her parents, her grandparents, and herself to end the fight once and for all. But . . . how could she possibly manage that without the key, when only four days remained before Rebecca reached her full human form?

"How are you holding up, dear?" Dorothy asked, sitting beside her on the couch.

"I'm okay. How about you guys? What are you up to with that vintage video camera?"

Her grandparents exchanged a glance.

"It was your mother's," Dorothy said.

Michele's mouth fell open.

"Marion and Irving met in a photography class. They both loved taking pictures and filming short movies," Walter explained, smiling sadly at the memory. "Irving seemed especially fascinated by the technology. The two of them liked to use the house and the grounds as a backdrop for their short films." He drew a deep breath. "We couldn't bring ourselves to touch Marion's room after she left, but once a year had gone by, we finally let the housekeeper in and she found Marion's camcorder. We tried to send it to her, but Marion returned every package and letter we sent, unopened. Irving had left by then, and she was no longer speaking to us. There was a tape inside the camera, but we . . . we couldn't bring ourselves to watch. It would have been too painful."

Michele sat bolt upright. "Wait—are you saying there's

footage of my parents together? And I can *watch* it?" In that moment, all the fear and frustration of the day evaporated. She couldn't remember the last time she had been so excited. "I get to actually *see* my dad as a real person, not just an old photograph? And Mom—I get to see Mom again!"

"I suppose we should have told you about it sooner," Dorothy admitted. "We assumed it might be difficult for you too. But now that you know everything . . . well, we thought it might be the right time."

Michele reached for the camcorder, smiling tremulously. "Getting to see my parents together, even if it's just on video— it means everything to me. Thank you so much."

Walter flipped open the small LCD display screen on the camcorder before handing it over. "The tape is from the early nineties, and we don't have the right cables for it to play on any of the TV screens in the house, but you can watch it right here on the camera. I charged it while you were at school, so all you have to do is press Play."

Michele gazed reverently at the camcorder in her hands. Even though she had never seen it until now, a rush of nostalgia flooded through her as she held the antiquated gadget. It was clearly a relic of happier, simpler times. Michele could almost feel her mother's presence inside the camera; she could practically see Marion running through the Windsor Mansion while peering into the lens, proudly making her own films at a time when home movies were newly in vogue. As she looked at the camcorder, Michele had an uncanny feeling that it had something to tell her.

"I can't believe I'm about to see my parents," Michele said in amazement. "Do you guys want to watch with me?"

The two of them shook their heads.

"It's still . . . too hard for us," Walter said quietly. "But we want you to watch it. You never got to see your parents together. You deserve that."

"Thank you. I can't thank you enough," Michele said fervently.

As soon as her grandparents left the room, she huddled on the couch, her heart hammering with anticipation as she pressed Play.

The tape began with static, so much so that for one awful moment Michele thought there might be nothing else—until the four-inch display screen lit up with the beautiful face of a youthful Marion Windsor. Michele's hand flew to her chest, her heart twisting at the sight. *"Mom."*

She looked so young, almost younger than Michele. Marion's auburn hair was pulled back into a ponytail, highlighting the exuberance on her face. She wore jeans and a pink T-shirt, and when she spoke, her voice was lighter than Michele had ever heard it.

"Time to go," her mother said excitedly into the camera. "He's waiting!"

Marion turned the camera away from her, showcasing Windsor Mansion as she tiptoed out of the bedroom and down the grand staircase. Her handheld flashlight served as the video's only form of lighting.

"I have to be very quiet," Marion stage-whispered into

the camcorder as she passed the Grand Hall and headed through a dark corridor. "Mom and Dad could seriously hear a mouse!"

She silently opened the door to the library and slipped inside. Michele watched in astonishment as young Marion tip-toed toward the glass-enclosed wall of books at the back of the room, and pushed her palms against it. The bookcase swung open, leaving a tall, gaping hole in its wake.

"Oh, my God!" Michele yelped as she watched the scene. What *was* that?

The camera zoomed in closer, and Michele saw that the hole in the wall was actually a dark tunnel lined with bricks, large enough to stand upright in. Marion crept purposefully along, the flashlight illuminating her way, until a second beam of light appeared and stopped Marion in her tracks.

"Baby!" she called, her voice filling with excitement.

He stepped into the light, and Michele gasped. It was her father.

Irving Henry gently took the camcorder from Marion and set it on a ledge before pulling her into an embrace, his flash-light clattering to the ground as he lifted her in the air. Michele's eyes filled with tears at the first glimpse of her parents together. The love she saw on the screen was so powerful, her parents so vibrant, it felt as if they were both alive again.

Michele gazed at her father in awe, unable to believe she was really seeing *him*, and not just staring at an ancient photograph. He was dressed in his best imitation of 1990s style: a Pearl Jam T-shirt paired with blue jeans and Converse sneakers. But Michele could still sense the Victorian young man he really was, from his proper posture to the old-fashioned tinge in his warm voice as he murmured Marion's name.

Goose bumps rose up her arms as Michele watched her parents onscreen, whispering and laughing together. Marion snuggled her head against Irving's shoulder as he wrapped his arm around her protectively. Michele couldn't get enough of seeing them together. As she gazed at her father, it occurred to her that he looked just like the Old Hollywood version of movie star Paul Newman, from his light brown hair parted to the side, to his clear blue eyes and earnest smile.

*That's my dad!* Michele marveled. Until now, she hadn't admitted how much of her life she'd spent wishing for her father. She had always longed to know what it felt like to be able to introduce friends to "Dad," to know that he would be there to pick her up when she fell, to walk her down the aisle when she married.

"I just want to be certain that you know what you're getting into." Michele heard Irving's urgent words and sat up straighter, watching the scene closely.

"Of course I do," Marion answered firmly. "I don't need any of this—not the money or the mansion, not any part of this life, if it means I can't be with you."

"But Marion," Irving said hesitantly, "you're still so young. What if you leave everyone and everything you've ever known, only to later discover that you don't like all you see in me?"

"Not this again!" Marion said, giving him a playful shove. "How many times do I need to tell you? I love you just the way you are. I'll never want anybody else."

"Are you sure?" he asked in a low voice. "Because if I had the chance . . . I would spend every moment of every day with you."

"That's all I want too," Marion said intently, and a smile flickered across her face. "When you start thinking like this, just remember our song."

"Which one?" Irving grinned. "You've only named everything on MTV this year 'our song.'"

"No—our real song," Marion told him, and she began to sing in her hopeless voice:

> *"Don't go changing to try and please me.*
> *You've never let me down before. . . ."*

Irving laughed and watched adoringly as she jumped up to perform in the middle of the secret passageway. Her unrestrained passion and pitchy singing made a sweet and hilarious combination, and Michele giggled through her tears as she watched her mother belt out off-key:

> *"I need to know that you will always be*
> *The same old someone that I knew.*
> *What will it take till you believe in me*
> *The way that I believe in you?"*

By the end of the song, Irving was in her arms, the two of them slow-dancing in goofy fashion as they sang the Billy Joel song together.

> *"I just want someone that I can talk to.*
> *I want you just the way you are."*

They finished the song in a heap of laughter, Irving kissing her hair as they embraced.

"You're the best thing that I've seen in this world," he told her fondly. "And believe me, I've gone far."

"Yeah, it's quite a trek from your place in the Bronx to Manhattan," Marion joked, flushing happily. Irving didn't respond, but Michele knew what he had meant. In his time travels across more than a hundred years, Marion Windsor had made the greatest impression of all.

Suddenly, black-and-white dots of static filled the screen. Michele's face fell as her parents disappeared, the sound of their far-off laughter echoing in her ears. It was a gift to see them together, even if only on videotape—but remembering that both her mother and father were gone, that the three of them could never be a family, brought forth an almost mind-numbing pain. Then Michele thought of the secret passageway in the video and felt a twinge of hope. Her grandparents must not have known about it; otherwise Marion and Irving wouldn't have risked getting caught there in the middle of the night. What if her parents had unknowingly left more clues behind?

Michele jumped off the couch, grabbing the small flashlight that she kept under the bed, and hurried downstairs to the library. Heart hammering in her chest, she moved toward the glass-enclosed wall of books. She had the sudden fear that her grandparents might have somehow learned about the passageway and sealed it shut.

*Please let it still be here,* Michele prayed. Holding her breath, she pushed against the glass, just as she'd seen Marion do in the video—and it swung open.

Michele clapped her hand over her mouth, watching the dark stone tunnel from the video materialize right in front of her. Her body trembled with nervous anticipation as she slowly climbed inside. She was immediately struck by the scent of a man's cologne . . . a classic scent. Something one might have worn in the nineteenth century.

"Dad?" she whispered, daring to hope. "Are you there?"

Proceeding farther through the tunnel, she flicked on the flashlight just before the darkness could envelop her fully. The thin ray of light was far from powerful, and she felt along the brick walls, using her hand to guide her.

"Dad . . . can you hear me?" she called out desperately, feeling slightly ridiculous. After what seemed like half a mile, Michele realized she had reached the end, marked by a small wooden door. Upon seeing it, she found herself looking up at the sky, breathing in the afternoon air. Holding the door open so she could get back into the passage, she craned her head and saw that she was below the ground of the Windsors' back lawn. *Who would build a passageway like this?* Michele wondered as she crept back inside. With a heavy heart, she made her way toward the library, feeling lonelier than ever without the animated, affectionate presence of her parents.

Suddenly, her foot caught on something. Michele held on to the walls to stop from falling and shined the flashlight toward the ground. She froze in place.

A box lay at her feet—a box with Marion's name written in old-fashioned lettering.

Goose bumps covered her entire body as Michele sank to her knees. She knew even before opening the box that it was from her father. With shaking hands, she lifted the lid and found three leather-bound books inside, with a yellowed sheet of handwritten paper at the top. The writing was so old and faded that Michele had to squint and hold the paper up against the glow of her flashlight to read the words.

*Dearest Marion,*

*I have lain in wait for you for twenty terrible days, from the moment I was forced back to a world that I can no longer stand to inhabit. I'm unable to do anything but stare at the door, expecting to see you run through it, and every moment that you don't is a moment that I curse myself for the decision I made. I live in fear of a life spent without you.*

*I see now that I made a horrible mistake by not confiding in you. I was certain that when you found the key, you would be brought here to me—and now I fear that I was wrong, that I have no way of reaching you. My only hope is you returning here to our secret place and finding the answers I've left. I pray every day that you will, and that once you read my story you might forgive me.*

*I am withholding nothing from you now. Here you will find out about me what I should have told you from the start. I know it will be a shock, and I apologize . . . I should have prepared you for this. Please believe me when I say that everything I did,*

*whether right or wrong, was to protect you and keep*
*you safe.*

*I love you, from here through eternity,*

*Irving Henry*


By the time she reached the end of the letter, tears had blurred Michele's vision. Her father must have never guessed that Marion would blame her parents for his disappearance and refuse to return home. She imagined him spending the rest of his life in agony, wondering and waiting for her. *If only Mom had seen this,* Michele thought, her throat tight with anguish.

She set the letter down and reached inside the box. The first item she retrieved was a leather-bound volume with no title on its cover. Michele curiously opened the book to its front page. *The Handbook of the Time Society.*

*What in the world is the Time Society?* She flipped to the next page, which was blank save for a sketch of a coronet circling a clock.

At the bottom of the box were two journals with Irving's name inscribed, the first one dated 1887–1888 and the second dated 1991–1993. Anyone else looking at the two journals would think they were a joke, that they could never belong to the same person. But Michele knew the truth.

*1888—that was the last time Irving and Rebecca were ever photographed together,* Michele remembered, quickly retrieving his 1887–1888 journal. She needed to find out everything she could—before it was too late.

## THE DIARY OF IRVING HENRY
### December 24, 1887—New York City

I arrive at Grand Central Depot in the midst of the Christmas-time chaos, watching as white-gloved porters swarm the well-to-do ladies and gentlemen in first class, eager to help with their monogrammed trunks and valises. No one pays me any attention, but I'm none too surprised. I'm used to fading into the background. As a butler's son, I've grown up knowing that my role in life is an inconspicuous one.

I find myself whistling "Oh Susanna" as I navigate the terminal, jostling through the crowds of men and women as they hurry onto different train platforms. The ladies' long skirts trail the floor in front of me, while children in their Christmas best struggle to keep up, clutching the hands of their nannies. Occasionally I spot a student like myself running to hop a train, and I tip my hat to one wearing a vest stitched with the logo of my university, Cornell.

As I open the doors leading to Forty-Second Street, I brace myself for the cold. Sure enough, there is a biting December wind, and snow flurries fall from the twilit sky. Hansom cabs and horse-drawn jitneys are hitched outside the station, and I jump into the first one available.

"Merry Christmas! Seven hundred ninety Fifth Avenue, please."

"Are you certain about that address, boy?" the driver asks skeptically.

"Of course I am," I reply, swallowing the familiar annoyance at the blatant surprise people always express when they learn that I know the Windsors personally.

"If you say so." The driver cracks the whip, and we're off! I grab hold of the inside door handle to keep from getting tossed across the carriage seat as the horse clip-clops at a fast trot over the cobblestones.

We make our way uptown, and I can't help smiling as we pass one brownstone after another with its lights aglow, decorated evergreen and fir trees sparkling from the windows. As we draw closer to Fifth Avenue, the roads become clogged with horse-drawn carts, wagons, and coaches, as well as pedestrians crossing in their holiday finery. At last I spot the majestic Gothic Revival structure of St. Patrick's Cathedral, and I know that we are almost at 790 Fifth. But at that moment my vision blurs. I blink a few times, and then open my eyes wide.

I am looking at an unrecognizable, unfathomable New York. Though I am still in the horse-drawn cab, still gazing out the window at St. Patrick's, the church now has two magnificent twin spires where none existed a moment earlier! Buildings stretch impossibly high, as if they are reaching for Heaven. The roads are a smooth concrete, no more cobblestone, and the vehicles on them are *self-powered*—no horses pull them, nor do they even need cable or rail tracks to run! These vehicles are unlike anything I have ever imagined. Meanwhile, the residential, exclusive Fifth Avenue has transformed into block upon block of unfamiliar shops and commercial buildings. Most shocking of all are the people, especially the young women. They walk the avenue unchaperoned, and actually wear *trousers*!

I squeeze my eyes shut. When I finally open them, the scene has returned to normal, and I breathe a sigh of relief.

I've been plagued by these visions ever since I was a little boy. Instead of simply seeing a town or a city as it is, I can somehow see it as it *will be*. I've never told anyone about the visions, not even my father when he was still alive. I was too afraid he would deem me mad. But I must admit there are times when I actually *hope* for the maddening visions to come and show me another glimpse of the future. I feel I am meant to be a discoverer, a scientist, and my most frequent lament is that I was born too early. I exist in too primitive a time period—I can't stand the thought of being left behind with the other ghosts of the nineteenth century, missing out on all the incredible advances and inventions that I sense are farther around the bend.

Moments later we reach Millionaires' Row, the stretch of Fifth Avenue where gargantuan estates stand in competition with one another. I can't help laughing aloud at a dreadfully ill-conceived few that are a mishmash of architectural styles, clearly built with the sole aim of impressing spectators rather than making comfortable homes. White Elephants, I remember my schoolmate Frederick calling these ostentatious mansions.

But when the hansom cab stops at Fifth Avenue and Fifty-Ninth Street in front of a pair of stately wrought-iron gates, I find myself speechless. I can't think of a single disparaging comment as I catch my first glimpse of the Windsors' brand-new home, which fills an entire city block! If only Father had lived to see this.

I spot two familiar footmen, wearing baroque eighteenth-century-style liveries and powdered wigs, stationed just inside the gates. Quickly paying my fare, I jump out of the hansom cab to greet them.

"It's awfully good to see you, boys!" I hurry toward them, beaming.

"Welcome back, Irving!" The older footman, Oliver, smiles with approval as he takes in my appearance. "University must agree with you. You're looking very healthy and well."

"Miss Rebecca will be *most* pleased to see you," teases Lucas, the footman my age who was my closest friend before I went away to school.

I shake my head at them, about to make my retort, when a formal carriage pulls up to the entrance. I glance at the two of them awkwardly. Normally, I would have been outside with them in matching liveries, an extra hand to help greet the guests. But tonight, for the first time, I am a guest, and it gives me an odd, out-of-place feeling.

"Go and have a good look at the house. It's quite incredible," Oliver tells me enthusiastically before he and Lucas return to their duties.

I walk through the grounds of the estate as if in a dream, taking in the gleaming white marble mansion. The four-story structure reminds me of the paintings I've studied at university depicting palazzos of the Italian Renaissance, and for a moment I imagine that I, Irving Henry, am in Europe! Loggias, balconies, and arched windows decorate the mansion's exterior, while towering white columns frame the entrance. As I make my way through the grassy front lawn and rose garden that lead to the front doors, I can tell before even stepping inside that this is the finest home the Windsors have ever built.

My first instinct is to look for the servants' entrance, until I remember Rebecca's insistence that I am to be her guest for the holiday, and that it "wouldn't be proper" for me to consort with the staff this week. I can hardly imagine how she managed to wangle this invitation from her parents, though I suppose they view it as a charitable gesture for the son of the butler who faithfully served them until his death. And of course, I know the money has turned me into a figure of some interest. It certainly isn't every day that a butler dies leaving enough savings to send his orphaned son to preparatory school and university.

I climb the steps hesitantly, wondering if it isn't too late to find the door to the servants' hall. But before I have a chance to retreat, the front door swings open and the new butler, Rupert, stands before me.

"Irving! Isn't this the nicest Christmas treat to have you back," he says happily.

I embrace him warmly. It's difficult to see anyone else in the position my father always held, but Rupert is like a godfather to me. He is in large part responsible for my change in circumstances. After my father died of a heart attack when I was a boy of thirteen, Rupert—then Mr. Windsor's valet—took me upstairs to see the master, holding a copy of my father's most recent will, written two years earlier. Mr. Windsor read the paper several times over, squinting in disbelief.

"*How in the world did he amass this kind of money?*" he demanded.

"*Byron saved up all of his wages, sir, all these years he's been here,*" Rupert had explained, his voice breaking as he spoke of my father, his friend. "*I knew him well and he rarely ever spent a penny; he invested everything with the bank. He told me he was saving for Irving to go to university. He wanted his son to be a gentleman.*"

Mr. Windsor was silent for a moment, then turned to give me a serious look. "*I will take you to the bank tomorrow, Irving. Once we verify the funds, I'll have you enrolled in a fine boarding school. You have no family named in this will, so you may return here for your winter and summer holidays for as long as you are in school. You can help the footmen with their duties in exchange for room and board.*"

I'd nodded with gratitude, though at thirteen years old I was unable to comprehend what this rapid change in my circumstances meant.

The final paragraph of the will was something none of us had understood. "*Equally if not more important than the funds for Irving's university education is the key that I leave for him, an heirloom that was very precious to me and will be to him as well. Please keep it for life, my son, only passing it to one of your children when it is time.*"

But none of us ever found a key, not even after searching and emptying my father's room and his deposit box at the bank. I'd never heard Father even speak of a key, and I wondered if that part of the will was some sort of metaphor, a symbolic message that I have yet to understand. I ponder it often. The words of his will sounded so urgent, how could the meaning behind them be so obscure?

I force my mind back to the present. "It's grand to see you too, Rupert. This new house is . . ." I shake my head, unable to find the words.

"Just wait, you haven't seen anything yet." Rupert grins. "Let me show you to your room." He takes my trunk from me, and as I start to protest, Rupert holds up his hand firmly. "The Miss wants you treated like a guest this holiday, and so you will be."

I sheepishly follow Rupert into the main entrance vestibule, which is enough to stop me in my tracks.

"It's a palace!" I exclaim, walking around the open-air indoor courtyard, which is decorated with marble columns, lush carpets, dazzling chandeliers, and silk draperies. A ten-foot-tall Christmas tree stands in full splendor in the center of the room, lavished with hundreds of twinkling lights and enchanting ornaments. As I breathe in its piney scent, I glance up and see the hallways of the second and third floors, framed by bronze railings and marble pillars.

"A palace is a very fitting description," Rupert agrees. "This room is called the Grand Hall. It is the central reception area of the house."

He leads me to the sprawling marble staircase and up two flights until we reach the rooms on the third floor. A dark wood balcony overlooks the floors below, and I stop to look down on the Christmas tree in the Grand Hall before following Rupert to my guestroom.

"The family's rooms are on the left, guest rooms to the right," Rupert directs. We walk through a long red-carpeted corridor until he finally stops in front of a white doorframe. "Here are your guest quarters."

I step inside, and for a moment I am too overwhelmed to speak. It's the nicest room I've ever had, with a colorful carpet filling the vast space, a double bed that looks cozier than anything I've ever slept on, a wooden chest of drawers, a bedside table with its own gas lamp, two plush armchairs, and various objets d'art.

"I never thought I'd stay in a room like this," I admit. "Bless Rebecca for her kindness."

"I don't know that anyone could accuse Miss Rebecca of kindness," Rupert replies, his tone sharper than I've ever heard it. I look up, startled.

"What is it? What's Rebecca done now?"

Rupert looks as if he regrets his outburst. "She gives the other servants a bad time," he says haltingly. "It's strange, when she's always taken such a shine to you. Though the ladies' maids have said on a few occasions that your face could make up for anything, even a lower-class birth." He laughs, and I shake my head with embarrassment.

A few minutes after Rupert leaves the room, I hear the sound of my doorknob turning. I glance at the door and see my oldest friend, Rebecca Windsor, dart inside, gazing at me with the excitable expression of an animal that has found its prey. I find myself taking a step back as I doff my hat.

"Merry Christmas, Rebecca! Jolly good to see you. But if someone were to find you in my room—"

"*I* don't care if they do." She gives a little turn around the room. "What do you think?"

"It's fantastic!" I enthuse. "I was just telling Rupert that it's like a palace. You must love living here."

"I wasn't asking about the *house*," Rebecca says scornfully. "I meant, what do you think of this?" She gestures to herself, dressed up in a cranberry-colored velvet gown with a large bustle.

I struggle for something to say. The truth is, Rebecca has never been pleasant to look at, from the paleness of her severe face to the sharp features below her heavy dark eyebrows, and black hair that always looks rather snakelike. Most people I know find Rebecca fearsome, with her harsh looks and sharp temper. I'm one of only a few who aren't intimidated by her.

I was just a baby living with my father in the servants' quarters of Rebecca's home when she was born. I was there when she walked her first steps, and to the general amazement of the Windsors and their staff, she singled me out to be her one and only friend when we were children. We played together, and then endured adolescence, always set apart by our social standing—though Rebecca never made me feel unimportant for being the butler's son. Instead she was possessive of me, and I could never help feeling flattered by her attentions.

"Well?" she presses, reaching for a compliment.

"You look lovely," I lie. "That dress is very becoming."

She smirks, squeezing my hand. "I have something quite unbelievable to tell you," she whispers. "It's a secret. You are likely to be the *only* person I will tell. It's the finest secret I've ever had."

My interest is piqued. "Tell me, then."

"Not yet. The dinner guests will be arriving any minute. No, I think I'll tell you after the party," she says with a mysterious smile.

The Christmas Eve festivities last well into the evening, and I nearly forget about Rebecca's big secret as I experience my first Windsor dinner party abovestairs. It's a small affair consisting of family and close acquaintances, but there is still an army of servants stationed throughout the mansion to tend to the guests. Mr. and Mrs. Windsor, Rebecca, and her older brother, George, are like the royal family greeting their subjects, standing by the Christmas tree in the Grand Hall to receive each guest before they proceed into the drawing room. Rupert announces their names loudly before they approach the Windsors, and when he calls out "Mr. Irving Henry," I feel my face turn bright red.

The drawing room looks like a temple of excess, from the fragrant flowers filling every corner to the exaggerated gowns and excessive jewels adorning the women and the gaudy gold pocket watches carried by the men. I stand alone in a corner, feeling uncomfortable and out of place as I watch my footmen friends pouring drinks. After half an hour, Rupert arrives and stands importantly in the doorway.

"Madame, the Christmas Eve dinner is served!"

I take Rebecca's arm and we follow the procession into the dining room, right behind George and his fiancée, Henrietta. "Isn't she an awful hag?" Rebecca snickers in my ear as we walk behind the two of them. I cringe, hoping they didn't hear her words.

The meal is a ten-course feast, beginning with oysters on the half shell followed by turtle soup, then striped bass in a heavy cream sauce and a Christmas turkey stuffed with truffles. Roman punch cleanses the palate before the next round of dishes: canvasback duck and a mixed lettuce salad. The final course is dessert, a tasty Christmas pudding followed by petits fours and plates of cheese and fruit. I only manage a few bites of each dish, never having eaten like this in my life, and I notice that nearly everyone else leaves their plates half-touched too. I suddenly feel queasy as I think of all the food that will be thrown out uneaten at the end of the night.

I listen with interest to the dinner conversation, hoping for nuggets of knowledge from the titans of real estate in the family. Yet the conversation is light and breezy, with the Windsors and their guests mainly discussing yachts, horses, and houses. I find myself itching for the company of the servants belowstairs—I know the conversation will be much livelier there!

While I watch the footmen bring round the endless courses, and listen to the chatter at the table, my mind ponders the way people in our Gilded Age equate wealth with freedom. But in this world, the wealthier are all the more trapped—like Rebecca, who I know is under pressure to find some sort of duke or count to marry. The wealthy Americans of our day are ensnared by their rules and rituals, hiding behind the European monarchs that they so desperately copy instead of forging their own identities. I wonder if this will remain the case in the decades to come.

At last, the end of the meal is signaled by the arrival of coffee and sparkling water. Mrs. Windsor leads the ladies into the drawing room, while we men linger at the table to smoke cigars and sip brandy. The men and women reconvene for a private recital of arias from Handel's *Messiah* to conclude the evening. Finally, when the last guest has departed and the Windsors are upstairs in bed, Rebecca sneaks into my guestroom to reveal her secret.

I sit in an armchair opposite Rebecca, unable to believe the words that are coming from my friend.

"Irving, I mean it." Her low voice is filled with excitement. "I can travel into the future! I don't know how it happened. I must have been *chosen* for this power." Her mouth curves into a smug smile. "I've done it twice already, and I have so much to tell you. New York in the future, why, it's even better than all those stodgy professors of yours predicted!"

"Rebecca . . . I'm afraid this is too much to believe," I say gently. And to think I'd been afraid that *I* might be called mad!

"I knew you would say that," Rebecca says dismissively. "Watch me."

She reaches up, pressing her hand against the high collar of her neck, and murmurs something inaudible. Suddenly her body *hovers above the room*. I bite back a scream, watching in utter shock as she spins like a tornado—and then disappears.

"Rebecca!" I whisper, terrified. W*hat* is *she*? My mind suddenly flashes back ten years, unearthing a memory I hadn't thought about in ages: that curious day in the park when the two of us saw the Vanishing Girl. Was Rebecca one of *those*?

She returns instantly, smiling triumphantly. Her hands, empty before her disappearance, are now clutching a piece of paper. "Well! Now do you believe me? I just spent two minutes in this same room in the year 1900."

I stagger backward in shock, unsure of whether Rebecca is the lucky time traveler she claims to be—or some sort of demon. She seems to read the fear on my face and rolls her eyes before handing over the wad of paper. I unfold it and see that it is a square ripped from a calendar. A calendar dated 1900.

I stare at her in stunned silence. This conversation has rocked the world as I know it; it's opened up endless possibilities, and now I feel my first flame of envy, the sudden all-possessing desire to have what she has. I know in this moment that I will never be the same—that from now on, I'd give anything to share in her power. *I* am the academic; I'm the one fascinated by the future. I know it's unkind of me, but all I can think is: It *should have been me instead*.

"Take me with you," I plead. "You know how much I long to see the future. Please take me with you."

Rebecca watches me with a self-satisfied expression. I know that she relishes this moment, the first time I've ever begged her for anything. Rebecca has always been power-hungry, with her place in society feeding her obsession. As one of the most prominent heiresses in America, she has all the trappings of power—but being a young woman in our time means she will always be ruled over by someone else, from her parents to her future husband. And so she savors any opportunity to hold others under her thumb, to show the world that *she* is in control.

"I don't know that I can," she answers slowly and deliberately. "I'm not quite sure that's how it works. But if it does, there's only one way I would take you with me. As my husband."

I nearly snort with laughter. She has to be kidding. But as I look at Rebecca's serious expression and hungry eyes, I realize with alarm that this is no joke.

"But Rebecca, you couldn't possibly expect your parents to ever let you marry me," I insist, trying to talk her out of this harebrained idea. "It would kill your mother to see you with anyone less than a baron."

"I don't need my parents' permission anymore, or anything else from them," Rebecca fires back. "I've been to the future, and I can go again and again, discovering inventions and banking secrets that I can bring back to our time. I'll make us a fortune and we will be independently wealthy, with no need to even be connected to the Windsors."

"What are you saying, Rebecca?" I stare at her in horror. "You mean to disown your family *and* make a dishonest living?"

"Only if I have to," Rebecca replies, shrugging.

I shake my head, aghast. "Why me? Why do all that to be with me, when you could have such an easier time of it with someone in your own station?"

"Because you're the only one who understands me, who

wouldn't try to control me," Rebecca answers candidly. "And I've always liked your face, ever since we were kids. You're the only person I've ever wanted to have."

And suddenly, the time-traveling heiress walks up to the middle-class butler's son . . . and kisses me boldly on the lips. My heart sinks as I realize I am trapped. I don't have the slightest romantic feelings for Rebecca, and the sensation of her lips on mine gives me a slight shudder. But then, her friendship certainly made my childhood in the servants' hall a far brighter experience. I especially remember her kindness after Father died, the way she shared all her newest games in an effort to distract me from my sadness; the way she convinced her parents to let her dress in black mourning clothes for a whole month after he died. There are far worse things than being married to my friend, and being able to travel or maybe even *live* in an evolved future New York makes it a worthy bargain.

"All right," I agree. "If you're sure. But I don't want us making a dishonest living. So we'll have to wait to marry until I've finished university and started work."

Rebecca flashes her teeth in a wide smile and pulls me close. It is only later that evening, as I struggle to fall asleep, I realize—I was *bribed* into making her a proposal. I know I shouldn't trust her, yet I can't resist following her lead. She bemuses and fascinates me, and though my pride prickles at the thought, I want to be like her. I want the power she carries: the ability to do the impossible.

Grounders are human beings who cannot travel through time. Ninety-five percent of the population falls into this category, blissfully unaware of the power and ability that forever eludes them. Hence, we Timekeepers never tell Grounders our secret. No good can come of it—only jealousy, resentment, and the desire to expose our Society.

A Timekeeper is required to keep his or her time-travel ability hidden from one's own family, waiting to reveal this gift only to the heir of the Key, just before passing away from the physical world. It may sound lonely to keep such a secret all your life, but know this: so long as you are in the Time Society, you are never alone. You're surrounded by people just like yourself—those who understand you in a way no one else ever could.

—THE HANDBOOK OF THE TIME SOCIETY

The chime of the nearby grandfather clock jolted Michele's mind back to the twenty-first century. She sat still for a long moment, her thoughts swimming with visions of a teenage Irving and Rebecca on their nineteenth-century Christmas Eve. She stared down at the journal, feeling a strange sense of betrayal, knowing that her father had been engaged to someone else in the family before her mother—someone as evil as Rebecca.

She slid the bookcase open and peered to check the time, jumping to her feet when she saw it was six o'clock. Walter and Dorothy would be expecting her for dinner. Gathering Irving's journals in her arms, about to step out of the passageway, she suddenly had a funny feeling that his box of secrets should remain in the tunnel. The diaries had survived this long in the passage . . . maybe it *was* the most secure hiding place, safer than Michele's bedroom. And what if, by taking the journals away, they would be gone when Irving checked in his Time? Michele couldn't bring herself to get his hopes up that Marion had finally found them. Reluctantly, she placed Irving's letter and diaries back inside before closing the panel.

As she made her way from the library to the dining room, her mind consumed by all she'd just read, Michele had a thought so startling, she nearly tripped over her own feet. If all had gone according to her father's plan, if Marion had been the one to find his journals and use the key . . . then *Michele would have been born in the nineteenth century.* In a way, her 1994 birth date was a mistake—a flaw.

She was still recovering from this realization when she joined Walter and Dorothy at the dinner table. The first course, a bountiful salad, was already set, but Michele wasn't sure she'd be able to eat a thing after the day she'd had.

"How was it?" Dorothy asked when she sat down.

For a moment Michele froze, wondering if they had some-how found out about the passageway and the diaries, until she remembered the video.

"It was so surreal and amazing to see them." Michele smiled at the memory. "I never thought I would ever get that chance. They were so happy and affectionate, singing and laughing. I want to always remember them like that."

"I suppose—you must think worse of us now," Walter said haltingly. "Since we were the ones to separate them."

"No. I might have thought that once, but not anymore. It was Rebecca who separated them. I'm convinced, especially after seeing that video, that my dad returned to his own time to protect my mom from Rebecca. Maybe he knew she would be in danger as long as he stuck around." Michele reached for her grandparents' hands across the table. "It wasn't your fault."

Walter squeezed her hand gratefully, while Dorothy blinked back tears.

"I never realized . . . how long I've needed to hear those words. That it wasn't our fault," she said quietly.

"I know my mom would agree," Michele said sincerely. "No one could have imagined the truth, but I know if my mom were here today, she would forgive you—and she would be sorry for all the years lost."

"When we learned that she named us your guardians, we actually thought . . . maybe she had forgiven us," Walter murmured.

"Maybe," Michele agreed. "I think she must have realized things were different than she'd imagined."

The three of them were quiet, each lost in their own thoughts. Michele wondered if she should tell her grandparents about the passageway and the diaries—they were sharing so much with her now, while she had managed to rack up a handful of confidences to keep from them. But then she remembered Irving's words in his letter: "*. . . our secret place.*" They clearly hadn't wanted Marion's parents to know about the passageway, and Irving never intended for them to read his journals. Michele felt a pull of loyalty to her father. She knew his secrets weren't hers to tell.

"Are you still sure about staying in New York?" Dorothy asked suddenly, a wrinkle of anxiety appearing on her brow.

"Have you given any more thought to getting away, like we suggested?"

Walter cleared his throat. "What Dorothy means is, we understand you want to handle this your way, but . . . you only have four days left and it doesn't seem like there's any sort of plan. If we hide you, at least we have some control in keeping you safe."

Now Michele was *really* glad she hadn't told them about the stolen key. They would have never let her out of their sight.

"I do have a plan. It just involves me finding out as much about my dad and Rebecca as I possibly can," Michele told them. *And, of course, getting my key back somehow,* she added silently. "I'm not going to run away; it won't solve anything in the long run. There's really nothing you can say to convince me."

Dorothy gave a resigned sigh and glanced at Walter. "Then I think we should call Elizabeth."

"I still don't see how she can help," Walter argued. It was clear they'd already had this conversation.

"She talks to the *dead,* Walter," Dorothy said urgently. "She can somehow . . . make a connection between Michele and Irving, before Michele risks going back in time."

"Okay, whoa." Michele held up her hands. "What in the world are you guys talking about? Who is this Elizabeth person who talks to the dead?"

"*Supposedly* talks to the dead," Walter clarified. "We have no proof that she's for real."

"Sure, but who is she?"

"Elizabeth Jade—she grew up with Marion," Dorothy answered. "They went to elementary and middle school together, but they lost touch in high school, when Elizabeth's parents sent her to boarding school in Massachusetts. We heard from the Jades that Elizabeth had some problems at school, and for a while she was being handed off to a series of different psychiatrists. But she always insisted that she *wasn't* crazy—she was a psychic medium. Her talents had flourished while she was away, and her classmates were naturally frightened when she could predict events and see the dead."

Michele listened with rapt attention.

"Her family turned away from her, of course. Here on the Upper East Side, the daughters of prominent families are expected to marry up and become the belles of New York society. The last thing the Jades wanted for their daughter was a controversial career as a psychic medium. But then, several years ago, Elizabeth was instrumental in helping the NYPD solve a kidnapping case and rescue the victim. From that moment on, she's been something of a celebrity. She just wrote a book on using self-hypnosis to awaken psychic gifts, and it hit the top of the *New York Times* bestseller list."

"She sounds amazing. I wish she and my mom had kept in touch," Michele remarked.

"Elizabeth called the day Marion died," Walter said, his voice low. "The girls hadn't talked in nearly twenty years, and for some reason on that day, Elizabeth thought of her and wanted to get back in touch."

"That's why your grandfather doesn't want to have anything to do with Elizabeth—she's another reminder of that terrible day." Dorothy looked gently at her husband. "But there's no doubt in my mind that she has the talent everyone says she has."

Walter heaved a sigh. "It's up to you. I don't agree, but if you want to talk to her, I won't stop you."

"I want to." The conviction in Michele's voice caught her by surprise. "Better yet, I want to meet in person. Let's set something up for as soon as possible."

## DAY FOUR

Before Michele knew it, November 19 had arrived: the night of the Autumn Ball. Part of her thought it was completely nuts to put on a fancy dress and attend a school dance in the middle of her crisis, when time was quickly running out, but she couldn't bring herself to let Ben down. Moreover, she needed to find another opportunity to talk to Philip—not to steal him away from his date, as much as she secretly wished she could, but to find out *how* he could see Rebecca, and what he knew. She had to find an excuse for a private moment with him at the dance, though after the choir-room debacle, she had a sinking feeling that he'd be avoiding her all night. *But if I can just get him to listen to me, to really* hear *what I'm saying and believe me, maybe then he'll open up and tell me the truth,* Michele thought hopefully. Her mind raced with visions of them banding together to defeat Rebecca, returning to the closeness they once shared and recovering Philip's memory along the way. Michele knew it was a long shot . . . but it was all she had.

Caissie arrived at the Windsor Mansion later that afternoon, lugging her dress in a garment bag and a tote filled with makeup, so the two of them could get ready together. The girlie scene was subdued, both quieter than usual. Caissie seemed moody as they styled their hair and makeup, while Michele was immersed in thoughts about her dad. The discovery of her father and Rebecca were the only aspects of her time travels that she'd withheld from Caissie. She hated keeping secrets from her, but she wasn't ready to explain the whole truth just yet. As great a friend as she was, sometimes she got a little *too* interested in Michele's time-traveling ability. Michele secretly feared that if Caissie knew she was a daughter of both the nineteenth and twentieth centuries, she would cease to be just her friend—and would become Caissie's science project instead. But she did confide in her about yesterday's encounter with Philip in the choir room and the loss of the key during the blackout, making sure to leave out any mention of Rebecca.

"What?" Caissie bellowed when she learned about the key, her exclamation so loud that Michele had a feeling they could hear her all the way to Brooklyn. She lowered her voice. "How—how could this happen? That key is only the most powerful object I've ever heard of—"

"I *know*," Michele groaned, covering her face with her hands. "It *kills* me that I don't have it anymore. I have to get it back."

Caissie bit her lip. "Sorry—I didn't mean to make you feel worse. Don't give up hope. You could still find it."

"I'd give anything for that to happen." Michele exhaled, watching as her normally low-maintenance friend fussed in front of the mirror. "Are you okay? Excited for your first real date with Aaron?"

"I would be, if he called it that," she said dryly. "He keeps referring to this as a friend-date. Not the most flattering thing to hear."

"I bet he's just nervous," Michele told her. "I mean, you guys have been best friends since freshman year, so he's probably a little freaked out about things changing. That doesn't mean he doesn't want them to change."

"I hope so." Caissie turned to face Michele. "How do I look?"

She wore a long, mint-colored halter dress, her shoulder-length strawberry-blond hair pulled back in a half-up half-down style. She looked beautiful, while still maintaining her quirky-cute style with silver feathered earrings and a matching hair accessory.

"You look perfect," Michele told her with a grin. "He's going to be all over you."

As if on cue, the intercom in her bedroom sounded and Annaleigh's voice piped through the speakers. "Girls, your dates are here!"

"Here goes," Michele said under her breath before grabbing her silver clutch and taking a quick glance in the mirror. She felt a chill of déjà vu as she looked into the glass. Her only Gilded Age–appropriate dress was the blue chiffon that she had worn to the 1910 ball where she first met Philip. Her appearance was a constant reminder of that night, a reminder that she knew would be all the more painful when she saw him with Kaya.

Ben let out a wolf whistle as the girls came down the grand staircase and Michele couldn't help noticing that he looked pretty cute himself. She glanced over at Aaron and was glad to see him do a double take at the sight of Caissie, giving her a shy smile before handing her a corsage. After Annaleigh posed them for some cute-but-corny photos, they piled into Ben's car and headed for the Waldorf-Astoria. The hotel was an art deco high-rise with over a century of history, and it suddenly occurred to Michele that Philip Walker might have attended events there in the early twentieth century.

The four of them walked through the main lobby, a two-story grand promenade reinforced with black marble columns. In the center was a tall antique clock, so spectacular that Michele had to stop for a closer look. The clock stood over nine feet tall, its gold surface ornately decorated with carved depictions of historical icons, from Benjamin Franklin to Queen Victoria, with a sculpture of Lady Liberty topping it off. The classic piece looked strangely alive, and Michele would have continued gazing at it if Ben hadn't pulled her away.

They followed the hotel's Peacock Alley promenade until they reached the Empire Room, a dazzling ballroom decorated in blue and gold. The coffered ceiling soared more than twenty feet above them, with antique French crystal chandeliers casting a glow around the room. A massive dance floor filled the space, and handsome oak tables at the back held vases of flowers, punch bowls, and trays of hors d'oeuvres.

"Wow. This is some dance," Michele remarked as she glanced out one of the towering arched windows, which reflected views of Park Avenue from behind rich damask curtains. Her eyes scanned the floor for Philip and Kaya, but they hadn't arrived yet.

"Everyone looks so . . . good," Aaron commented, his eyes roaming approvingly over the girls, who had clearly taken to the Gilded Age theme, displaying lavish dresses that seemed to be slinkier, form-fitting renditions of the classic ball gown. Caissie rolled her eyes, nudging him in the ribs. "Come on, Aaron."

A full jazz band was stationed on a second-floor balcony. As Michele and Caissie handed their wraps to a coat check girl, the musicians launched into a fiery cover of Nina Simone's "Take Care of Business," complete with horns, castanets, and a singer who emulated Nina's smoky voice.

"Is this what they would have played at a real Gilded Age ball?" Caissie asked Michele doubtfully.

"Hardly," Michele laughed. "Must be the band's idea of it. But this is definitely more danceable than what they played back in the day."

She and Caissie couldn't help giggling as they watched their classmates attempt to dirty-dance to the incompatible jazz music.

"Fakin' Jamaican alert!" Caissie stage-whispered with glee, as the school's two blond wannabe-Rastafarians swaggered onto the floor, bobbing their heads and moving to the beat like they were attempting a rain dance.

"This night just might turn out a little better than I thought," Michele said, looking on with amusement at the Fakin' Jamaicans' shenanigans.

And then, suddenly, she felt her body tense, and goose bumps rose up her arms. She couldn't see him, but sensed his presence. Michele turned around, and sure enough, there was

Philip, walking in with Kaya on his arm. For a moment, Time froze. Kaya and everyone else at the dance vanished, leaving Philip and Michele alone in the ballroom. Dressed in a tux, with his hair slicked back and the signet ring glimmering on his finger, he had never looked more like the Philip Walker she fell in love with one hundred years in the past. She noticed that he looked unnerved, and when his eyes fell on Michele, his expression intensified.

"You ready?"

Michele glanced up, Ben's voice breaking the spell. The sounds and sights of the dance once again filled her senses, and she found herself now staring at Kaya, looking gorgeous in her low-cut strapless rose dress.

"Sure." Michele followed Ben onto the floor as the band struck up the Gershwin classic "They Can't Take That Away From Me." As the singer began the first verse, Philip and Kaya followed them. While they danced with their respective partners, Michele and Philip locked eyes.

> *We may never, never meet again on the bumpy road*
>    *to love.*
> *Still I'll always, always keep the memory of . . .*

Michele looked away, a lump rising in her throat. As soon as the song ended she turned to Ben with a forced smile. "I'm going to get a drink. Do you want anything?"

"I'm good. Want me to come with you?"

"No, that's okay," Michele told him. "Do your thing, I'll be right back."

She had just reached the punch table when piano chords that were all too familiar filled the room. She whirled around, staring up at the band in the balcony. Were they *actually* playing it?

> *Feels like so long been only seeing my life in blues*
> *There comes a time when even strong ones need rescue*
> *Then I'm with you in a whole other place and time*
> *The world has light,*
> *I come to life . . .*

Michele's mouth fell open in amazement as she watched her classmates sway and dance to the song she and Philip had written one hundred years ago. She found herself looking for Philip among the sea of faces, but couldn't spot him. And then she felt the tingling brush of someone's hand against hers. He was right behind her.

"What happened yesterday, with the sheet music?" Philip blurted out in a low voice. "And what is this song they're playing now? Why does it remind me of . . . you?"

Michele felt her heart nearly stop. She turned around to face him. "You—you remember?"

Philip's blue eyes darkened with frustration. "No, I just . . ." His voice trailed off as a few of their classmates walked up to the table, glancing at the two of them oddly. "Come with me."

Michele could barely breathe as she followed Philip out of the ballroom and back into the main hotel lobby, away from the Berkshire students. They slowed in front of the lobby clock.

"It's like déjà vu," Philip continued, his words tumbling

out in a rush. "Things seem familiar that I *know* aren't. And I feel different than I should—" He broke off suddenly, looking like he regretted his admission. For a moment they were both silent, Michele's mind whirring. Faint strains of their song wafted through the open doors of the Empire Room.

> *Why, when you're gone,*
> *The world's gray on my own*
> *You bring the colors back*
> *Bring the colors back . . .*

"What's going on?" He looked at her desperately. "Everything's turned upside down since I moved to the city, and I don't know why, but somehow . . . I know it has to do with you."

"I wish I could tell you everything, but I'm afraid you'll think I'm crazy—even crazier than you probably think I already am," she said with a shaky smile. "We have so much to talk about, but first, you just need to *remember.*"

"Help me, then." Philip moved a step closer to her, and Michele felt a delicious shiver run up her spine at the feel of his breath on her cheek.

Summoning her courage, Michele took his hand, lacing her fingers with his. "Does this . . . feel familiar?"

Philip held his breath. He closed his eyes, and for a minute the two of them seemed to have forgotten where they were.

"Michele," he whispered, as if in a trance. "I don't know why I feel like this."

She found that she could barely move or think as Philip

gently leaned his forehead against hers, his body so close that she could hear his accelerated heartbeat. With trembling hands, she reached up and placed her palm against his, their fingers interlacing again. Gazing at each other, a look of mutual understanding seemed to pass through them, when suddenly the grand lobby clock struck—and Michele felt their two bodies begin to rise.

Philip drew a sharp breath, clasping her hand tighter and looking down in disbelief as their feet were lifted off the floor by an invisible hand. *"What's happening?"*

Michele was too stunned to respond, looking around wildly as an indoor wind filled the lobby, swirling itself around them. She heard Philip's yell mingling with her own cry of shock as they clutched each other, their bodies spinning together through the air.

*It feels just like time travel,* Michele thought frantically. *Only it* can't *be. I don't have the key—and I was never able to travel with Philip when I tried before. What* is *this?*

She watched with a mix of terror and awe as the room's appearance shifted rapidly in a kaleidoscope of images, and for one split second it seemed they had soared through the ceiling and into the night sky, until they hurtled toward the ground, landing in a heap on a parquet floor. Michele heard a soft moan beside her.

"Wh-what the hell—I'm losing my mind—" Philip's voice stammered.

Michele felt something slip out of her grasp. Philip's hand was no longer in hers. She turned to face him—and drew back in shock. *He was gone.*

"Philip!" Michele screamed, scrambling up off the floor. But her voice was drowned out by the sounds filling the ballroom: the strains of an orchestra playing a waltz, the din of laughter and chitchat, shoes clattering as dancers weaved across the room, glasses clinking, the sweep of heavy skirts and trains.

"Oh. My. God," Michele whispered, staring at the scene in front of her. It was undeniable: she was in another time. But *how*? And where was Philip?

She circled the ballroom in a daze. While it seemed like she had returned to the Empire Room of the Waldorf-Astoria, lit by the same French chandeliers and sconces, everything else was vastly different. The contemporary decorations from the Autumn Ball had disappeared, replaced with gilded mirrors and European tapestries framed by garlands of ivy. Everywhere Michele looked, she saw a profusion of flowers—waterfalls of orchids, potted palms, and roses adorning the chandeliers and scattering along the outskirts of the dance floor. Even the second-floor balcony, where a classical orchestra played instead of the twenty-first-century jazz band, was festooned with colorful roses and plants.

Ben, Caissie, Aaron, and all the rest of Michele's classmates had vanished, their places taken by a more formal crowd from another era. Instead of the teenage boys reluctantly clad in tuxedos, these were stately gentlemen all dressed in the same white ties and black tails, with white gloves adorning their hands. And while the Berkshire girls had worn sleek dresses with minimal fabric, these ladies waltzing were attired in low-necked, heavy gowns of brocade and velvet, embellished with eye-popping displays of jewelry.

Michele weaved through the crowd, invisible to the ball guests as she searched for Philip. She nearly wilted with relief when she finally spotted him, but then felt a jolt of surprise at the sight of him chatting languidly with two other young men—as if he belonged there.

Philip turned in her direction and his eyes widened, his face breaking into an incredulous smile at the sight of her. He was still dressed in the same tux that he'd worn to the Autumn Ball, yet his expression revealed to Michele at once that this was Philip from the past—the Philip who remembered and loved her.

He hurriedly excused himself from his friends and signaled Michele to follow him into the corridor. She found herself running toward him, heart racing with anticipation. When they both reached the quiet corridor off of the ballroom, he threw his arms around her, jubilantly lifting Michele into the air, before burying his face in her neck as he held her tight.

"I'm so happy to see you," he murmured.

"Me too," she whispered.

Lowering his head, Philip leaned in closer, gently brushing his lips against hers. Michele held him tighter, her knees weakening and her stomach flip-flopping ecstatically from the sensation of his kiss. She wrapped her arms around his neck, kissing him back fervently. It felt like forever since they'd been together like this.

"How long has it been since you last saw me?" she asked breathlessly, when they finally managed to break away, flushed and exhilarated. "What's today's date?"

"November 19, 1910," Philip replied, twirling her around

playfully. "It's only been one week, but I've missed you terribly all the same."

*November 19, 1910—that was just before we separated,* Michele realized. *He doesn't know yet that Time will force me to say goodbye.* The thought brought sudden tears to her eyes, and she blinked them away, anxious to forget everything else, to simply hold on to this blissful moment with Philip in 1910.

"I've missed you too. More than you know." She pulled him into another embrace, closing her eyes as he kissed her hair. They clasped hands and walked farther down the corridor, unable to stop smiling at each other.

"Is this the Waldorf?" Michele asked.

Philip nodded.

*That means I didn't just travel back in time—I traveled to another location,* Michele marveled, remembering that the original Waldorf was located on what would be the site of the Empire State Building after the 1930s.

"I'd been dreading coming here tonight, for the Vanderbilt Ball. It's been so difficult for me to act as I did before you came into my life, going on with the same mundane frivolity," Philip admitted. "But you know what they say: once you accept an invitation to a dinner or ball, only death can excuse you from the commitment—and even then your executor must attend on your behalf." Michele giggled, and Philip grinned back. "Thank God I came. I wouldn't have missed seeing you for the world."

The orchestra struck up Schubert's *Serenade,* and Philip and Michele exchanged a glance, laughing softly.

"That's our cue." He held out his hand, and Michele's

fingers intertwined with his—just as she had done with twenty-first-century Philip's earlier that evening, in a future Time and place. As they began to waltz, faces pressed close together, it seemed they had both escaped the constraints of Time and the physical plane. All that existed was this: a love so strong it seemed to lift them off their feet, carrying them into another world.

"What is this?"

Michele turned around at the sound of Kaya Morgan's voice. *What was she doing in 1910?*

Michele dropped Philip's hand in shock as she saw a pale-faced Kaya standing with a small group that included Ben Archer, a pained look on his face. They were back in the Waldorf-Astoria lobby, standing by the grand clock—the last place they'd been before transporting to 1910.

"We're back," Philip murmured dazedly.

Michele gasped, turning to him in hopeful astonishment. Did that mean . . . that the new Philip remembered being there with her in 1910?

"Seriously, Philip. What happened to you?" Kaya's eyes flashed as she looked between him and Michele.

Philip suddenly seemed to snap back to the present.

"I— Let me explain." He gave Michele a quick glance, then stepped away from her, leading Kaya out of the lobby. As she watched him go, wondering what sort of explanation he'd come up with, she spotted Ben stalking away, his shoulders slumped. Michele hurried after him, back into the Empire Room.

"Hey." She grabbed his arm. "I'm sorry. I don't know what you saw, but—"

"I saw you and the new guy getting pretty damn close and dancing like old-fashioned weirdos," Ben snapped. "What happened to that long-distance boyfriend you told me about? Seems like he disappeared awfully fast."

Michele knew she couldn't very well tell Ben that Philip Walker and the "long-distance" boyfriend happened to be one and the same.

"We were just . . . waltzing," she told him instead, her face flushing as she realized how ridiculous that sounded in the twenty-first century. "Besides . . . I thought you said you were cool with going as friends."

Ben exhaled. "Yeah. I guess I did," he said evenly.

The jazz band chose that moment to segue into a bouncy, peppy rendition of the Depression-era tearjerker "Brother, Can You Spare a Dime." After a few moments of silence between them, she couldn't help remarking, "This is a pretty odd song choice for a school dance."

The corners of Ben's mouth twitched. "I don't think they're exactly preaching to the choir here," he said, gesturing to the privileged sons and daughters of New York surrounding them.

Michele laughed. She knew she had been forgiven.

"Come on, let's dance," she said, pulling him toward the parquet floor. Michele's heart felt lighter than it had in weeks, her hand still warm from Philip's touch, her lips still tingling from his kiss.

*"I saw you and the new guy getting pretty damn close. . . ."*

As Ben's words echoed in her ears, Michele found herself

grinning with delight. This *proved* that Philip of 1910 and Philip of 2010 were the same.

As they circled the floor, Michele noticed Caissie making her way to the punch bowl alone.

"Hey, where's Aaron?" Michele asked Ben.

Ben peered over the top of her head and pointed. He was dancing with some girl Michele hadn't seen before.

"I'm going to go check on Caissie," Michele told Ben as the song ended. She was dying to tell her friend what had happened too.

"What's going on?" she asked once she reached her.

"That sophomore has study hall with Aaron," Caissie said numbly. "She asked him to dance, and he asked me if I minded. Of course I wasn't going to tell him no! But it's been three dances in a row now."

Michele groaned. What was he *doing*?

"I'm so sorry, Caissie. He's just being immature. How were things going with you guys before?"

"Pretty good, actually." Caissie bit her lip. "We were having fun, but it was different than when we normally hang out. It felt exciting. And then . . . he decided to go dance with another chick."

"That's so weird." Michele looked across the ballroom at Aaron, puzzled. "I wonder if he just got nervous. You should talk to him, casually ask him if everything's okay."

"I don't know, I just want to avoid him at this piont. Distract me, please. How's your night going?"

"Are you sure? I think avoiding him will only make things more awkward," Michele advised.

"I don't know what to do. But I don't want Aaron looking over here and guessing that I'm all upset over him. So c'mon, tell me about your night." Caissie took a sip of punch and looked at her expectantly.

"Well, it's been kind of unbelievable," Michele said into her ear. "Philip remembered our song when the band played it—and then we went to talk alone, and somehow we went back in time to 1910! The old Philip was there and we were a couple—and when we were jolted back to the present, the new Philip *remembered* that we'd been somewhere else. It wasn't just me imagining things or traveling on my own!"

"Wait, *what?*" Caissie screeched. "Are you serious? What does it *mean*? And how could you go anywhere without your key?"

"I have no idea. I almost don't know whether to believe we really, physically traveled back in time—or if it was, I don't know . . ."

"Like a shared vision or something?" Caissie suggested, furrowing her brow in thought. "I guess that could be possible in your trippy world! So what happened with Philip? Did he say exactly what he remembered?"

"No, Kaya and Ben were there when we . . . got back. He went to try to explain things to her, and I haven't seen either of them since." Michele scanned the crowd.

Just then, Nick Willis from their English class approached Caissie and asked her to dance. Caissie looked over at Aaron, still dancing with the sophomore, and firmly took Nick's hand.

"I want to hear this story again, with way more detail, when I get back," she called over her shoulder before joining Nick.

As Caissie disappeared into the whirl of dancers, Michele's eyes lighted on Philip escorting Kaya into the room. Both of their faces looked shaken, but Kaya had a bright smile frozen on her face.

Though Michele and Philip didn't have another moment alone for the rest of the night, there was a new energy between them whenever their eyes met across the dance floor. Michele sensed that the veil was finally lifting—and a new chapter was just beginning between them.

Age Shifting is the art of traveling through time in the body of your younger or older self. This is a highly advanced Timekeeper skill, one that involves both practice and conviction. Once you've mastered age shifting, you will be able to move through Time in the body of your choice, which becomes especially valuable as you age. Heart disease, chronic pain, and weak bones—they all disappear when you age shift into the body of your younger self. However, caution must be advised. Much as we need sleep for our bodies to function, we also need time to "rest" in our true age. Age shifting takes quite a toll on the body, and spending too many days being younger or older can limit your total life span. Yet if used moderately, this skill can have the opposite effect, adding years.

—THE HANDBOOK OF THE TIME SOCIETY

Michele practically floated home after the dance, glowing as she greeted Walter and Dorothy. Her grandparents attributed her happiness to a successful date with Ben Archer, and she didn't bother correcting them. When she finally made it to bed, Michele lay there for what seemed like hours, too keyed up to sleep. As the clock ticked later and later, she realized this was the perfect time to continue her father's story. So she slipped out of bed, flashlight in hand, and crept down to the library and the secret passage within it.

## THE DIARY OF IRVING HENRY
### *January 1888—New York City*

Now that we are secretly promised to one another, Rebecca has made it crystal clear that she expects me to pay her a visit at least once a month. It's quite a journey from my university campus; there are no direct trains to the city from Ithaca, so I must travel to Pennsylvania first and then hop another train to Manhattan. Still, I arrive as promised a few weeks after Christmas and find Rebecca nearly jumping out of her skin in eagerness to share some news. She clutches a leather-bound journal possessively in her hands.

"I was paid a fascinating call today," she boasts. "Millicent August—isn't that the most intriguing name? Well, you will never begin to imagine who she is!"

I plop into a chair, instantly grumpy. Every time I have to hear about one of Rebecca's extraordinary adventures, my alter ego of envy rears its head. I can't understand why I must be stuck in the provincial 1880s when I could be in the future like Rebecca, learning medical and scientific marvels. I keep trying to remind myself that as soon as we're married, she will take me—though it grates on me that she's pulling my strings this way, keeping me hooked with the promise of time travel. But the promise alone is tempting enough to hold me to my position as Rebecca's reluctant fiancé.

She leans forward, unable to hold in her news any longer. "Millicent August is almost *one hundred* years old, though she looks no older than my mother, and she is the leader of the Time Society. It seems there is a whole entity of people out there, just like me. I don't know whether to be upset that I'm not the only one or pleased that I now have people on my level to associate with."

I sit up straight, paying full attention now. "So others can do it too? Did you ask her how?"

Rebecca pauses before responding. "It's called the Time Travel Gene. People know if they have the gene, just as I do." She gestures to the book. "Millicent gave me this handbook filled with information on the Time Society, and only members are allowed to see it. There are all sorts of rules and things, she says." Rebecca rolls her eyes. "But the main reason she came to call was with an invitation. There is a grand hotel being built in San Diego, California, called the Aura. Everyone else thinks it's simply a luxury hotel, but the truth is that one of the builders is a Time Society member, and the hotel is our new headquarters—"

I reach out my hand. "Please. Can I read it?"

"Irving! I told you it's for members only."

"We're to be married, though, aren't we? And husband and wife share everything." As the words leave my mouth, I suddenly hate myself for getting extricated in such an unholy engagement. But I can't help it. I'm desperate to see the future.

"Perhaps when we're married, you can join the Time Society too," Rebecca offers, tucking the book close to her. "But until then, I'd better not go against Millicent's wishes."

I look at Rebecca with narrowed eyes. It's typical of her to brag about something she has, only to guard it jealously. And then it occurs to me that Rebecca never takes orders from anyone; in fact, she detests authority. Her poor mother had a nightmare of a time trying to discipline her, and gave up in the end. It just isn't in Rebecca's character to follow the rules of this Time Society. I know in that moment—there has to be more to the story.

I descend the grand staircase alone, having just managed to wriggle out of Rebecca's suffocating goodbye embrace. As I reach the bottom step, my hair mussed and face still fixed in a grimace, I fail to notice Rupert at the foot of the stairs until the butler clears his throat.

"Oh—hello, Rupert. I'm just about to go into town to catch a train back."

"You're planning to return here often, aren't you?" Rupert gives me a knowing look. "Even after graduation."

"What do you mean?" I ask sharply. Does he *know*?

"I mean that Miss Rebecca always gets her way," Rupert says pointedly. "As your friend, I had hoped for a better sort of girl for you—though I can understand your reasoning for being with her. But if you are going to be living in the Windsor Mansion, there is something in this house that I feel I ought to show you. You might find it gives you an escape when you need one."

Rupert moves in the direction of the library, and I shuffle behind him. My face burns with shame as I realize he must somehow know that I plan to marry Rebecca and clearly don't love her. He must think I'm doing it for the money and status, and the thought makes me cringe with disgust. If only I could tell Rupert the truth!

We quickly reach the library, my favorite room in the new Windsor Mansion, with its floor-to-ceiling shelves and glass-enclosed cases filled with books upon books. Prized artwork and regal furniture also decorate the library, but I only have eyes for the hundreds of leather-bound tomes.

Rupert gives the room a careful once-over, then moves toward one of the glass bookcases at the back of the library. To my surprise, the always-polite butler pushes his hands against the bookcase rather roughly, as if trying to move it!

"What are you doing?" I ask, bewildered. "You'll break—"

I stop mid-sentence, my mouth hanging open as the bookcase mechanically swerves to the side, revealing a vast empty space that resembles a tunnel. I step closer and see that it *is* a tunnel built of gray stone and brick, and just high enough to stand upright in.

"What *is* this?" I exclaim.

Just as quickly as he opened the passageway Rupert closes it, nervously glancing at the front door of the library as he pushes the bookcase back in place. "It's a secret passage that leads to the back lawn of the house. For a space consisting of mere stone and brick, with no heat or decoration, it is a surprisingly comfortable place to get away for a bit." Rupert smiles, and then his expression turns serious. "No one else knows about it, especially not the family, so I must ask that you keep this a secret. I'm sharing it with you because I feel you might need it one day. Miss Rebecca is rather vile to all the staff here, and while she is enamored with you now . . . you don't know if one day she might become cruel to you too."

I lower my eyes. "It's not what you think. I—I'm not—I mean, I might not—" I stammer, before Rupert interrupts me.

"You don't need to explain," he says kindly. "You're eighteen years old and you want a better life. I understand."

For a moment, I'm ready to blurt out the truth. After all, Rupert just shared a secret with me. But then I imagine his reaction, the way he would likely panic and think I've gone insane. After all, without Rebecca's cooperation, I have no proof.

Suddenly, a question occurs to me. "Rupert, if the family doesn't know about this passageway . . . how do you?"

"It was the architect's secret. He loved putting his own private stamp on the homes he built, adding things to the house plans to show that it was *his* creation, despite whoever might own it. I was charged with supervising the building of this place while the Windsors were all staying at the Fifth Avenue Hotel. That's why, aside from the construction crew and now you, I'm the only one who knows about the architect's secret addition. The crew never saw or spoke to the Windsors; I'm the only one who could have told them. When the architect asked if I planned to tell, I knew instantly that I wouldn't." He looks at me guiltily. "I suppose that makes me an inferior butler, but I needed this. You see . . . I have a lady too, and here is the only place where we can be together." He drops his eyes, and I bite back a smile. I *always* had a feeling there was something between him and Rebecca's pretty French maid!

"I understand." I place my hand on Rupert's shoulder, about to say more, when a vision fills my mind, so powerful that it brings a searing headache along with it.

*I'm standing in the middle of the secret passageway, waiting for someone. My palms are sweaty, my stomach jittery, and yet I am happier than I have ever been before. I look down, carefully examining my clothes. I hope that I look all right in this strange outfit of blue trousers and a cotton shirt bearing the block-lettered words "New York Giants 1991." I chuckle at the thought that over a hundred years in the future, the fashion is to look plainer than the poor of my day.*

*Suddenly I hear the scraping sound of the bookcase being pushed to the side. My heart lifts, and I try in vain to control the smile spreading across my face. She is here.*

"Irving? What's happening? Are you all right?"

I snap back into focus as Rupert shakes my shoulders frantically.

"I'm fine," I gasp. "I just had a—an awful cramp in my leg. It's gone now." I look toward the secret passageway in awe. My heartbeat picks up speed as I realize that *it's going to happen.* I *really* am going into the future, and not just to 1919 like Rebecca—I'm going to travel more than a hundred years!

"Thank you for sharing this," I tell Rupert. "I have a feeling that I will need a secret passageway. Thank you."

As we leave the library, my mind races with one question: Who is the girl in my vision—the girl I will be waiting for in 1991?

*February 2, 1888*
I awake at six a.m. on the morning of February the second a far different person than I will be by the end of it. My eyes open upon my familiar, small, and stark dormitory room at Cornell University. I dress quickly, and then hurry to the washroom to shave before my first class. When I return a few minutes later, I see a *woman* sitting at my desk, watching the door, waiting for me.

I stare at her, stunned. Girls are strictly forbidden in the boys' dormitories—how had she made it past the warden? And this is no girl, but a woman, who looks foreign and ethereal, with waist-length silver hair and penetrating green eyes. She smiles at me.

"Irving Henry. I've wondered for a while when I might get to meet you."

I glance nervously from her to the door, and after a moment's hesitation, I close it behind me. I have to know who this woman is—but I can't risk any of my schoolmates seeing her.

"Who are you?" I demand. "What do you mean by this, breaking into my room?"

"Oh, I didn't break in," she says calmly. "Your door was open."

"How do you know my name? And, I repeat—*who are you*?" I stand with my back against the door, close enough to make a quick getaway if the woman turns out to be, as I suspect, certifiably mad.

"My name is Millicent August. Perhaps you've heard of me." She gives me a perceptive look as she holds out her hand.

My jaw drops. "Millicent August? The founder of the Time Society?"

"That's the one."

"What do you want with *me*? Is this about Rebecca?" I ask, perplexed.

"I'm here about both of you," Millicent says softly. "You see, there are some things that don't add up about Rebecca's circumstances. For instance, did she tell you *how* she is able to travel into the future? Did she tell you that time travel is an inherited gift?"

"No." I look at Millicent with wonder. "She said she was chosen for the power—that there is a Time Travel Gene and she was born with it."

Millicent chuckles quietly. "Of course. That is what she wants you to believe."

Now Millicent has my complete attention.

"What are you saying?"

"It's true that there is a Time Travel Gene, and it runs in families. But it's not quite so simple. People don't suddenly wake up one day and are able to visit the past or the future out of nowhere," she said in an admonishing tone, as if I were the one who suggested such a thing. "There is a device. A key."

"Rebecca didn't say anything about a key," I say, confused.

"No, she withheld that from you, and I believe I know why. Let me explain to you how time travel, and our society, works." She gestures for me to have a seat.

"The Time Society is a clandestine organization of time travelers. We call ourselves Timekeepers. Over the past century we have learned that the power to travel through time runs in a family's blood. This is what we mean by the Time Travel Gene," Millicent divulges. "But we are all marked by a physical key, called the Key of the Nile. This key is always given by the Timekeeper to one of their kin before they die. Thus, time travel is not something you are simply born with, as Rebecca said, but rather an inherited gift.

"Now, every single member of the Time Society is related by birth to another Timekeeper, which explains how we receive our keys. So you can imagine my surprise when our Detectors informed me of a new time traveler in our midst, Rebecca Windsor. You see, no one from her family has ever been in the Society. But there *was* someone else who lived in her house, who was a registered Timekeeper. Someone whose kin I was expecting." Millicent pauses. "The Timekeeper's name was Byron Henry."

For a moment I think my heart must have stopped beating. When I finally find my voice, it is barely a whisper.

"You're mistaken—that's impossible! My father was the most blessedly normal man you could imagine. There's no way he could have been—he would have told me—" I break off, my mind racing at a dizzying speed as I suddenly remember the portion of my father's will that no one had understood. "*Equally if not more important than the funds for Irving's university education, is the key that I leave for him . . .*"

"I know how close you and your father were," Millicent says kindly. "But you were too young to be told. One of the strongest guidelines we abide by in the Time Society is keeping our powers secret until we're nearing the end of our lives. Then we may tell the person who is to inherit the key. Of course, most of us cannot predict when we will die, which is why the last will and testament is crucial to our Society."

I wipe my brow, perspiring from all this astonishing news, as Millicent continues.

"I hadn't heard from Byron in a long while, but I never assumed he'd died. Some of our members can go for years without being in contact with us. But my suspicions were aroused when I heard about Rebecca and confirmed when I went to see her and found that the Windsor butler was no longer Byron Henry." She leans forward. "I am convinced that Rebecca stole the key from your father when he died."

I feel myself recoil. "But—but she is my friend. She wants

142

us to be married! I wouldn't put it past her to do something horrible, but not toward me. She knows how much I loved my father. She *couldn't* have stolen from him."

"I'm afraid it all adds up," Millicent says. "Especially since she wouldn't tell me who gave her the key. She feigned ignorance, but I know she stole it. I could see it written across her face."

My hands ball into fists as I feel an unfamiliar rage burn through me. "So you're saying that all this time she was boasting to me about time travel, telling me that I could only experience it through her, *if* I married her—was all a lie? The power was really meant to be mine all along?"

"Yes," Millicent says intently. "We always knew you would be the next Timekeeper in the Henry family. After Byron died, the only time traveler living in the Windsor Mansion should have been *you*."

I can't sit still anymore as the anger inside me escalates. I jump up furiously. "I have to get the key back. I have to get it away from Rebecca!"

"That's right," Millicent agrees. "I have invited her to the opening of the Time Society headquarters today. She will walk straight into our path, wearing your key." Millicent holds out her arm. "Are you ready?"

"I am."

"We aren't traveling very far, only to this afternoon, so the journey will be brief." Millicent unties her shawl, revealing a glittering gold chain tied around her neck, from which a large skeleton key dangles. A diamond punctuates the center of the key's surface.

"Hold on to the key," Millicent instructs me, and I nervously reach out my hand to touch it.

"The Aura Hotel. Five p.m. on February the second, 1888," Millicent commands. Suddenly, an invisible hand yanks me by my collar, pulling me into the air with breathtaking force. I feel my body rise higher and higher, then begin to spin at the speed of light, until before I know it, I am on the ground again, doubled over and gasping for breath.

"Here you are. You did very well."

I look up and see Millicent holding out a glass of water. I gulp it down, and then, catching my breath, I glance around at my surroundings. We are in a formal drawing room, complete with gilded ceilings and Louis XVI furnishings. Millicent approaches a large bronze clock framing the wall, and presses her hand against it. The clock chimes loudly, the sound seeming to reverberate throughout the space.

"They'll be bringing Rebecca in any moment now," Millicent says nonchalantly. "You'd best wait in the next room—we don't want her to see you too soon and make an escape. You'll be able to hear us through the wall and will know when to come in."

I nod, the anticipation of what lies ahead filling my body with renewed energy. I step into the adjacent room, Millicent's study, and glance at the books lining the shelves. I'm startled to see Millicent's own name on the spine of many of the titles, from *The Art of Age Shifting* to *The Gift of Sight*.

I soon hear footsteps and then Rebecca's excited voice as she greets Millicent. The sound sends a wave of nausea flooding through me.

"Hello, Rebecca," I hear Millicent say coldly. "Hiram and Ida, thank you for your help. You may go now." A moment later, after the drawing room door has opened and closed, I hear Millicent's voice again. "There's someone here to see you, Rebecca."

My cue. I turn the door handle that leads from Millicent's office into her drawing room and stare accusingly upon my former friend.

"*You!*" she gasps.

As Rebecca stands frozen in shock, Millicent reaches over and rips something off her neck. Rebecca cries out, but it's too late. Millicent presses the key into my hands, and I gaze at it in awe.

The golden key looks like an ancient talisman. It is carved in the same ankh shape as Millicent's, only instead of a diamond at the center, my key has a sundial etched on its surface.

"My father *drew* this for me," I tell Millicent, unable to take my eyes off the key in my hand. "He made me a drawing of this very key when I was a boy. I always thought it was just another one of his funny little sketches. But he was giving me a clue." I look up, glaring at Rebecca with hatred. "Perhaps he knew you would steal it, that one day I would be called upon to recognize it."

"I didn't—I didn't steal," Rebecca stammers, looking flustered for the very first time in all the years I've known her. "He left it in *my* house."

Her words make me tremble with fury.

"When did you take it from him?" I demand, stalking toward her. "He would have said or done something if he knew it was missing. So when did you take it? As soon as they buried him in the ground?" My voice rises and I find myself shouting at her, wishing my words could inflict the pain of physical blows.

Rebecca doesn't deny it, and I have to hold on to the back of a chair to keep from striking her. "So it's true, then. While you knew I was crying for my dead father, you were stealing from him. Stealing what was most precious."

"I wanted to feel closer to you, Irving!" Rebecca wailed. "You must know I've always fancied you. I knew how much you loved your father, and I wanted something to remember him by."

"That's a lie, and you know it!" I roar. "If that were true, you would have told me about the key, *shared* it with me, instead of boasting about your sudden time-traveling powers and bribing me into marrying you so that I could experience what was rightfully mine all along—what you had stolen from me!"

"Bribe you into marrying me?" Rebecca echoes, as if she didn't hear the rest of what I'd said. "Is that how you took it?"

"Of course. I have no more romantic feeling for you than I do for a teaspoon," I spit. "I never desired you, never! But I was your friend, a true friend. Far more than you ever were to me."

Rebecca's face turns a deadly white. She blinks quickly, and I'm astonished to see actual tears in her eyes. Rebecca never cries. But I turn away from her, knowing they are just the crocodile tears of an actress trying to extract what she wants.

A buzz sounds in the room, and a moment later two guards appear in the doorway.

"Thank you for your prompt arrival, gentlemen. Please search Miss Windsor's purse and pockets, and then escort her back to New York," Millicent instructs them. "Take her home by train. She is a thief and a fraud."

Rebecca's face turns monstrous with anger. "You have no right to do this! I am *Rebecca Windsor*! My father could—"

"Your name means nothing here," Millicent firmly interrupts her.

One of the guards pulls a leather-bound book out of Rebecca's handbag and hands it to Millicent. She smiles as she gives it to me. "I believe this belongs to you."

It is *The Handbook of the Time Society*. By now Rebecca is kicking and punching her fists at the guards as they hoist her out.

"You'll regret this!" Rebecca screams at me. "You'll regret making an enemy of me. I swear I'll destroy you!"

"Go on and try," I seethe. "There is nothing more you can do to me."

The guards drag Rebecca away and her cries grow fainter, until they are all but gone. I sink into a chair, suddenly exhausted.

"Thank you," I tell Millicent. "Thank you for rescuing my father's legacy. I wish I had known sooner who he really was. Now . . . I just hope to do him proud."

Millicent places a hand on my shoulder. "I believe you will. You are one of us. You are a Timekeeper."

*W*hile most time travelers are thrilled to discover their power, soon cherishing it above everything else, a small few shrink from the gift. To be different from the majority is often thought to be "wrong," and some misguided Timekeepers look upon their ability as proof that they are an aberration. This couldn't be further from the truth. We Timekeepers are gifted and chosen. *You* reading this are gifted and chosen. Always remember.

—The Handbook of the Time Society

*9*

Michele gaped at the journal in her hands, unable to believe the words written on its pages. Just as Irving's life had forever changed on the day he met Millicent August and learned the truth, so too had his story now altered Michele's world. She could barely comprehend all the facts, from Rebecca's ugly deeds to the knowledge that she and her father were a part of something so much larger than she'd ever guessed. There was a whole *world* of time travelers out there, others who'd experienced what she had! Her heart raced as she imagined taking a trip to the Aura Hotel and meeting the other Timekeepers. And to think that all along, the Time Society headquarters had been so close to her former home in Los Angeles.

*The Timekeepers can tell me what happened to my dad,* Michele realized. *They can help me find him!* But then she felt a wave of despair come over her, remembering that her key was gone. She'd lost the only ticket to reaching her father, misplaced his most precious possession.

*What about the fact that I went back in time tonight at the dance?* she wondered, jumping to her feet in the tunnel and pacing hopefully. But as she thought about it, Michele realized there had to be another explanation—like the shared-vision theory Caissie brought up. If she really *could* travel without the key, then she would have been transported to 1888 while reading her father's journal, just as the key had sent her to Clara Windsor's time of 1910 while reading her great-great-aunt's diary months ago, and then to Lily Windsor's time of 1925 when she discovered her great-grandmother's lyrics from the era. No . . . the power to time travel was within the key. And she had lost it.

"I'm so sorry, Dad," she whispered into the silence. Her stomach churned at the thought of Rebecca taking her revenge and stealing the key yet again. Although Philip said the creature hadn't touched Michele in the choir room, she knew it was no coincidence that someone stole her key right when Rebecca appeared. The thief must have been working for her.

Yet a huge piece of the puzzle was missing. If Rebecca had been cast out of the Society, with no key to bring back her power—then *how* did she ultimately end up a traveler? By what means could she have tormented Walter and Dorothy from beyond the grave and stalked Michele and Philip? How could she look like a teenager, how was she able to do *anything* when she should be powerless and dead in the ground?

Michele reached for the *Handbook of the Time Society*, wondering if this manual of magic held some answers. She closed her eyes, realizing this book had been right there at the Aura Hotel, in the center of the confrontation among Irving, Millicent, and Rebecca. So much had come and gone in the one hundred and twenty years since. It was incredible to look at this book and know that it had survived everything and was now here in her hands. She flipped it open and began skimming the words, too eager and impatient to read it properly, though she knew she would need to soon.

Her eyes lit on certain phrases as she thumbed through. "Age Shifting" was the title of one of the chapters, and her jaw dropped as she read the first sentence. *"Age Shifting is the art of traveling through time in the body of your younger or older self."* She read the sentence over again, wondering if it *really* meant that people in their forties or fifties could travel through time in their twenty-year-old bodies—and vice versa.

The following chapter was titled "The Visibility Paradigm," and revealed that *"in order to appear as a solid, visible human being and effect change in another time, you must spend seven straight days in the alternate time period before your body leaves its true present and joins you in the past or the future. Until then you are invisible, appearing only to those who possess the Gift of Sight. However, in our Society, remaining in another time past the seven days is forbidden. See the Four Cardinal Laws."*

Her adrenaline spiking, Michele quickly looked through the book until she found a definition of the Gift of Sight: *"The ability of ordinary human beings to see spirits and time travelers.*

*This is generally an inherited gift. The Gift of Sight flourishes among the young with a broad imagination, and can occasionally falter and fade as one grows older."*

Michele gasped. Now she had the answer to the question she'd been wondering about for weeks: why she had appeared invisible in the past, unseen by everyone except the Windsor girls and Philip. The Gift of Sight clearly ran in the Windsor family, and Dorothy and Philip possessed it as well.

The heading of the last page caught Michele's eye: THE FOUR CARDINAL LAWS OF TIME TRAVEL.

Timekeepers are not to interfere in Life or Death. Terrible consequences have followed when this warning has gone ignored. Your signature on the membership papers indicates your understanding of the Four Cardinal Laws below. You agree that failure to comply with these Laws will result in your immediate removal from the Time Society and forfeiture of your Key.

1. You shall never commit murder.

2. You shall never attempt to bring deceased persons back from the dead. This includes traveling to the past to stop a death from occurring.

3. You shall never conceive a child when in the past or future, NOR conceive with someone from another Time. This results in time-crossed children who cannot fully belong to any true Present, and who will go on being split between their father's and mother's Times.

4. To avoid these catastrophic outcomes, and to keep from tampering with the Natural Timeline, you

*shall never stay in any Time besides your true Present for longer than seven straight days. You shall not reach full Visibility in any time other than your own.*

Michele felt her heart jump into her throat as she read the third and fourth laws—both broken by her father. The words seemed to swim together on the page, blurring before her eyes, and a cold wave of fear gripped her insides. *I wasn't supposed to be born,* she thought, panicking. What did Millicent August mean when she wrote that time-crossed children "go on being split between their father's and mother's Times?" What was the *catastrophic outcome* that lay ahead for her?

Suddenly Michele felt claustrophobic. She had to get out of the tunnel—she needed air. After hastily stuffing her father's journals and the *Handbook of the Time Society* back into their box, she stumbled out of the passageway.

Michele slipped away through the Windsor Mansion front doors and into the night, breathing in shallow gasps as she looked around at a world that no longer made any sense. She pushed past the gates and broke into a run, forcing aside thoughts of her grandparents and their likely panic upon discovering her missing at this late hour. Any shred of security that she'd felt in her life had now been turned upside down, and she needed to run, to drown out the unwanted knowledge clouding her mind.

Michele ran so fast that the Manhattan landmarks and scenes seemed to move and transform beside her. As she raced past the glittering Plaza Hotel, the limousine parked in front of the hotel's entrance shook until it was no longer a limo, but a formal horse-drawn carriage. Michele blinked rapidly as she continued down Fifth Avenue, nearly falling over when she saw that all the modern-day buildings and shops had disappeared. Bergdorf Goodman and Henri Bendel, Abercrombie & Fitch, the Gap—they were all gone. Instead, those commercial blocks were now lined with extravagant houses similar to the Windsor Mansion.

*It's just my imagination,* Michele told herself. *I can't be in the past.*

Picking up speed, she crossed from Fifth to Sixth Avenue, the streets still in a time warp, with no trace of modern cars or buildings. Michele spotted a ghostly, lone newspaper boy hawking the day's paper, and she peered closer at the boldfaced date: November 29, 1904.

*Impossible. I don't have the key.*

She hurried down Seventh, not slowing until she spotted the hulking brownstone structure of the Osborne Apartments. As she came to a halt, everything around her returned to normal. Yellow cabs resumed their places, contemporary high-rises re-formed in the sky, and the marquees overhead hyped the newest Broadway hits.

Michele took a deep breath, looking at the Osborne with surprise. She hadn't realized she'd been running to him—and yet now that she was there, she couldn't imagine being anywhere else. She took a hesitant step closer and glanced up at his window. The curtains were drawn.

A wave of exhaustion swept over her, and before turning around for home, Michele looked back up at Philip's window once more. She gasped as a hand appeared, pulling back the curtains. A face pressed against the window and Michele's jaw dropped as grown Philip from the 1930s looked out into the night, his expression dreamy.

"Ohmygod." She was officially hallucinating. She blinked, and when she looked back the curtains were drawn once again. If only he'd *really* been there. With one last, longing glance, Michele backed away from the Osborne and turned toward home.

## DAY FIVE

Michele took a nervous sip of water as she glanced out the window of Celsius, the glass-enclosed restaurant overlooking Bryant Park and the ice-skating rink. The New York Public Library's mammoth Beaux-Arts structure stood just behind the rink, and part of her wanted to run out of the restaurant before her guest arrived and hide out among the books. But then a woman in her late thirties stepped inside, her green eyes warm and welcoming, and Michele felt herself relax.

"You must be Marion's girl." The woman greeted her with a smile. "I'd know those eyes anywhere. I'm Elizabeth Jade."

"Hi." Michele stood to shake her hand, but Elizabeth wrapped her into a hug instead.

"It's so lovely to meet you. I'm just . . . so terribly sorry about your mother." Elizabeth's eyes filled with sadness, and in that moment Michele sensed the friendship her mom and Elizabeth had once shared.

"My grandfather told me you called the day she died," Michele said. "What made you reach out after all those years?"

"I thought about her often. It wasn't just that day," Elizabeth explained, sitting across from Michele at the table. "We just changed so much in our teens. I went off to boarding school and developed this psychic ability that at first turned me into a loner. I was frightened and overwhelmed, and it was so much easier to be alone than to try to act like a normal teenager with my friends. By the time I was settled and confident with my new life, Marion had moved to L.A. It seemed like the window of our friendship had closed, but I missed her. I missed those days."

Elizabeth reached into her purse and pulled out a photograph, sliding it across the table for Michele to see: a picture of twelve-year-old Marion and Elizabeth, dressed in matching fluorescent jumpsuits with side ponytails. As she looked at the photo Michele found herself giggling and, at the same time, fighting back tears.

"Children of the eighties," Elizabeth remarked with a slight smile. "We had so much fun together." Her smile faded. "The day your mother died, I woke up with a horrible knot in my stomach. Her name was on my mind, and though I knew she was most likely still in L.A., I called your grandparents because they were my only link to her. All I wanted was to hear your grandfather say that everything was fine, that Marion was happy and safe in L.A. Which he did . . . but then, we all read the story in the paper."

Michele nodded, looking away. She couldn't stand to hear any more about the worst day of her life, and Elizabeth sensed this, quickly changing the subject.

"I want to hear all about you. Your grandmother tells me

some pretty . . . incredible things. If I were anyone else I might not believe her, but then, I'm the last person who's allowed to doubt someone's supernatural experiences." Elizabeth grinned wryly.

Michele took a deep breath, for a moment doubting how much to tell Elizabeth. But as she looked from the sweet photograph to the kind woman across the table, Michele found herself blurting out the whole story—from her romance with Philip in the past to the appearance of the new, modern-day Philip; her discoveries about her father and her identity as a time-crossed accident of birth; and of course the threat of Rebecca. By the time Michele finally finished, the wide-eyed expression on Elizabeth's face had her wondering if she had been too quick to open up to her mother's friend. What if this was too much madness for even a psychic medium to accept?

But then Elizabeth smiled broadly, reaching over the table to squeeze her hand.

"Of course Marion Windsor would have a daughter as incredible as you," she marveled. "Don't for a moment think of yourself as a mistake. Your parents fell in love for a reason, and I believe it was because you were *meant* to be born. There is no such thing as accidents in life. Great things will come of your abilities—I can feel it."

Michele felt tears of relief well in her eyes, and this time she didn't fight them.

"Thank you," she murmured, wiping her eyes. "I don't know if I can believe all that yet, after what I've read in the *Handbook of the Time Society* so far—but you've given me some hope."

"I'd like to put you under hypnosis at my meditation studio tomorrow, if you're comfortable with that. I believe your subconscious is very powerful—strong enough to show us answers as to how you're supposed to defeat Rebecca," Elizabeth said.

Michele hesitated. "Hypnosis sounds so . . . intense. What's it really like? What will happen?"

"It's nothing to be nervous about," Elizabeth assured her. "I'll simply guide you through deep breathing and meditation to help temporarily shut off your conscious mind and awaken your subconscious, to show us what you need to know. The hypnosis will last about thirty minutes or less, and then everything will return to normal. I promise you'll be safe."

"Okay," Michele agreed. "I'm in."

"Good. Now, as far as the tale of the two Philips. Did your mom ever tell you about the book she read in eighth grade, *The Reincarnated Soul*?"

"It doesn't ring a bell. Sounds like a pretty serious book for an eighth grader to read." Michele smiled fondly as she looked down at the picture of her mom as a precocious twelve-year-old.

"It was. I'm the one who recommended it to her," Elizabeth admitted. "The book was the firsthand account of Dr. Daniel Ross, a respected psychiatrist from Johns Hopkins, who worked with children who could recall their former lives. He worked with a toddler whose first words were in Gaelic instead of English, a teenager who remembered his entire life as a fighter pilot in World War II, and many other similar cases. Dr. Ross believed that we are all reborn after we die, and while we might have a new body and a new existence, our spirit stays the same. This explains the common phenomenon of déjà vu, as well as the feeling that we've known someone for a long time when we've only met them recently." Elizabeth paused. "I believe—in fact, I feel quite certain—that the current Philip Walker is a reincarnation of the same Philip Walker you had a relationship with in 1910."

Michele nearly choked on her drink.

"Wait, *what?* Are you serious? I'm just managing to wrap my head around time travel and being the daughter of two times, and now you want to add in reincarnation?"

"I can understand it sounding crazy to you. But there are many people out there who make a strong case for the existence of reincarnation. It would explain so much about you and the new Philip, including why your presence brings up feelings and fragments of memories for him, rather than him clearly remembering who you are and your relationship," Elizabeth explained. "Because it's rare for people to recall their past lives in detail, without undergoing past-life regression."

Michele let out a slow exhale, taking in all of this incredible information.

"He promised he would find a way back to me," she confided. "Is this what he meant?"

"A century ago, people knew even less about reincarnation than they do now. However, Philip's intention to return to you must have stayed with his spirit beyond his death, causing him to be reborn at a time when you two could be together. The theory of reincarnation is that souls with unfinished business return not just to earth, but to the same people they knew in previous lives. Philip obviously had unfinished business with you, and he chose to live again. He chose you."

Michele tried to speak, but couldn't. Elizabeth patted her hand understandingly.

"I know. It's a lot to take in, even for someone who's experienced as much as you have. When it comes to the paranormal, there's rarely a way to collect scientific proof, so at the end of the day you have to trust and believe what feels right."

"This does feel right," Michele spoke up. "It's unbelievable, but . . . it feels like the answer I was looking for."

Returning home, her mind filled with Elizabeth's words, Michele headed straight for the secret passageway. If Philip really did come back for her, then she had even more motivation to fight—and to stay in the present. She opened Irving's diary to the page where she'd left off, ready to learn all that she could.

# Aura Hotel

## San Diego, Calif.
## 1888

Epoch
Clothiers

Lobby

Currency
Exchange

Library

Theater

# Headquarters
## of the
# Time Society

President's
Drawing
Room

Sundial
Salon
Restaurant

President's
Office

## THE DIARY OF IRVING HENRY
### *February 2, 1888*

Millicent August smiles as she hands me a thin stack of papers, each stamped with the Time Society symbol of a coronet circling a clock. "Once you've signed these contracts you will be formally inducted into the Time Society."

I scrawl my signature and feel a flash of unexpected sorrow. *Nothing will ever be the same again.* The innocence of youth disappeared the moment I discovered the truth, and my former life vanished along with it. I'll never again be Irving Henry, the happy-go-lucky university student who considers the downstairs rooms of the Windsor mansions my home, who has a family in Rupert and the rest of the Windsors' staff. For the first time, I am truly on my own. I know it's for the best, and of course I realize that this newfound gift is the great adventure I always wanted—but still, I find myself wishing I could cling to boyhood just a little longer before facing the unknown world alone.

"I imagine you won't be returning to the Windsor Mansion," Millicent says, as if reading my thoughts.

"No," I answer firmly. "I'll never live there again."

"And what about university? Will you return to Cornell?"

"I'm not certain what I'll do," I admit. "All I know is that my old life doesn't fit anymore."

Millicent nods understandingly. "Yes. I can see that. Well, all Timekeepers are welcome to stay at the Aura for as long as they need. Would you like to reserve a guestroom? You can begin your first mission right away—your initiation. While in the coming months you will be assigned different years to visit and protect, your first mission is simply to *learn* the ins and outs of time travel, in the date of your choice."

My heartbeat quickens as I remember my vision from the secret passageway.

"Yes, I would like to start straight away. And I already have a date and place in mind." I take a deep breath. "1991 New York."

Millicent's eyebrows rise. "Any particular reason?"

"I want to go as far into the future as my mind can imagine," I answer, which is rather true.

"You will require preparatory help with this mission," Millicent cautions. "One of our Timekeepers who calls 1991 the Present will coach you before you make the time leap. We always have to be careful of those with the Gift of Sight when we travel, which is why we must assimilate into different time periods and not draw attention to ourselves. 1991 will be like an entirely different world for you."

"I can do it," I say boldly, though inside I'm beginning to feel my first flicker of nerves.

Millicent smiles. "If anyone can pull off an impressive feat, I imagine it might be you." She pauses. "There's something else you ought to know about your father. Byron was one of the few Timekeepers, along with myself, who was powerful enough to time travel without a key. He was rather famous in the Society because of it."

I stare at her, speechless.

"Are you all right?" Millicent asks.

"I—I thought I knew my father so well," I reply, when at last I find my voice. "He was always my hero, but I thought he was just a simple, good man—my father, the butler. Why wouldn't he tell me about all of this? And what perplexes me all the more is why he would go and work as a servant when he was an all-powerful time traveler. It doesn't make sense."

"He wanted you to be normal for as long as possible. That's what most of our Elders want for us before we are exposed to time travel. My grandmother was the same with me when I was young," Millicent confides. "Besides which, being the butler to a family like the Windsors is a fairly prestigious position."

I nod slowly. "Will I—will I be able to do it, too? Travel without a key?"

"It's unlikely. We haven't yet found two Timekeepers within the same family who can both travel keyless. But there are other gifts I expect you will uncover," she says, her eyes crinkling as she smiles at me.

Moments later I am alone in the Headquarters library, surrounded by a pile of books to prepare for my first mission. While I eagerly flip through *The Mechanics of Time Travel*, I hear the sound of the door opening. A young woman walks in, wearing an outfit so bizarre, it reminds me of my Christmas Eve vision of an alternate Fifth Avenue.

She is dressed in pale blue denim trousers, something only *cowboys* wear in my Time, with a blindingly bright orange T-shirt under a denim jacket. Her shoes are unlike any I have seen, a strange combination of canvas and rubber. Oddest of all is her hair, which is tied like a horse's tail to the back of her head. The girl notices my blatant staring and chuckles.

"I take it you've never seen anyone from my Time before." She approaches me, holding out her hand. "I'm Celeste Roberts, born 1975 and coming from my Present of 1991."

"What?" I gape at her.

Celeste peers more closely at me. "Wow, you're *really* new, aren't you? This is so exciting!"

I nod self-consciously.

"Okay, tell me your name, when you were born, and what Time you're coming from," Celeste instructs. "That's how we greet all Timekeepers we haven't met before—so we can keep track of who everyone is and what Time they're truly from."

"Oh. All right. I'm Irving Henry. I was born more than a century before you, in 1869, and I *am* in the Present—1888."

"Wow," Celeste breathes. "You've been dead for *ages* where I'm from!"

170

"And *you're* technically not alive right now," I retort, shaking my head with amazement. "This is some incredible magic, isn't it?"

"Seriously," Celeste agrees. "So I hear you've chosen 1991 for your initiation mission! It's a bold choice, but you're in for a treat. The nineties are a *blast*. I'm here to prepare you for the dramatic changes ahead, so let's get to it!"

I follow Celeste through the vaulted hallways of the Headquarters, trying to keep up as she chatters away. "It's not just new clothes that you need. You'll have to get a haircut immediately—you look way too old-fashioned. Short and parted off to the side, that's how all the attractive guys wear their hair in the nineties. And remember, if you're approached by anyone with the Gift of Sight, always go by Henry Irving instead of your real name. No one your age would ever be called Irving."

"All right," I say uncertainly, as we reach a whimsical tri-level boutique called Epoch Clothiers. Mannequins in the windows model the widest variety of clothing imaginable, from Elizabethan dresses with matching ruffs, colonial-era riding uniforms, and ball gowns and tuxedos from my century, all the way to women's dresses that cut off as high as the *thigh*, and men's sports clothes that look like they were designed for outer space.

I hold the door open for Celeste and as we enter, a tiny woman flits before us, wearing a long empire-waist dress and clutching a measuring tape in her hands. Her hair is a curly blond bob and her eyes look almost lavender.

"Hello! Welcome to Epoch Clothiers. I'm Lottie Fink, born 1863. What can I help you with?"

"I'm looking for clothes to wear in 1991," I tell her, feeling my pulse race at the thought. This isn't just a daydream anymore.

"Ah! Now that is a request I don't hear every day," Lottie says with a smile. "Follow me upstairs."

As we pass racks of clothing, I suddenly remember that all of my money is in New York.

"I don't have any money with me," I mutter to Celeste. "I should go—"

"Don't worry, that's common here," Celeste reassures me. "All Timekeepers have an open tab at the Headquarters, and we're billed twice a year. You can even borrow 1990s dollars from the Currency Exchange and they'll just add that to your tab."

I exhale with relief. "The Society thinks of everything, don't they?"

Lottie stops in front of a collection of eccentric-looking clothing, handing me a stack of plain cotton shirts in a variety of colors and three pairs of blue denim cowboy trousers similar to Celeste's. "Jeans and T-shirts—these will be your wardrobe staples in the 1990s," Lottie declares.

*Jeans*. So that's what they're called. I look up at Lottie in surprise.

"Men and women both wear these . . . jeans? And where are the sleeves to the shirts?"

Celeste laughs. "They're T-shirts, they're supposed to have short sleeves. And everyone wears jeans in the nineties—old people, kids, guys, and girls. The only difference is that us girls wear them tighter and guys wear them baggier."

Lottie lifts the lid of a shoe box and shows me a pair of white rubber and canvas shoes with the word "Adidas" written on the side. "These are called sneakers, and you can wear them almost every day with jeans."

Celeste holds open a shopping bag and I place the items inside, still eyeing the funny articles of clothing with amusement. Lottie darts among the racks and returns moments later with a pair of tan pants and a navy blue jacket, another shoe box under her arm.

"For more formal dress, you can wear these khaki slacks and a blazer over one of your T-shirts, with this pair of brown leather shoes."

"He should have a black leather jacket too," Celeste tells Lottie. "And a couple of Tommy Hilfiger sweaters."

Nearly an hour later, I walk out of Epoch Clothiers unrecognizable from the man who first entered. After choosing my wardrobe, Lottie led me to the barbershop at the back of the store, where a barber cut my wavy hair short and shaved my mustache, giving me a boyish appearance younger than my nineteen years. Instead of my three-piece Victorian suit and bowler hat, I now wear Levi's jeans and a black T-shirt, with a rounded-top hat that Lottie calls a "baseball cap." I feel strange and stiff, like I've stepped into someone else's skin, but Celeste grins at me approvingly as we leave the store. "*Much* better!"

Celeste leads the way to the wood-paneled lobby, an enormous space with a ceiling that stretches as high as the eye can see. "There's your last stop," she says, nodding at the Reservations desk. "Millicent already reserved Room 1991 under your name, so all you have to do is pick up your key and take the elevator to the ninth floor."

I look at Celeste gratefully. "I don't know how to thank you for everything. I would have been lost in all of this if it hadn't been for you."

Celeste grins. "Oh, it was fun. It's been a couple years since this world was new to me—it's been kind of exciting to see it through your eyes." She gives me a warm hug. "Good luck in 1991, and call me if you run into any trouble. You can find my number in the yellow pages under Brick, New Jersey."

"Yellow pages?" I echo. But Celeste has already disappeared.

I turn the key to Room 1991, my hands trembling with anticipation as I wonder what I'll find inside. I remember Millicent's words from earlier that day.

*"Each room here at the Aura is designed to fit a different time period, filled with the décor, literature, and papers of the day. This is to help us assimilate into the era we are traveling to. For example, if I am traveling back to the year 1750, I would spend the night in Room 1750, studying all the documents and artifacts from that year that our Researching Committee has collected."*

I hear voices inside my room, and I quickly switch on the lights. My legs nearly buckle from what I see.

A tall beige armoire stands opposite the bed, its shelves

open, revealing a black-framed screen inside. And there are real, live *shrunken people* within the screen, people speaking to me and laughing loudly, their clothes and hair and faces all in color.

I race up to the screen. "Who's there? Who are you? What is it you want?"

But the miniature people inside the box, a family of some sort, don't seem to hear me. They continue their chatter, while booms of laughter echo from somewhere unseen. I gingerly reach up to touch the screen and gasp as I feel nothing more than a shiny, hard surface. A book is propped up against it, with the title *Television Manual*, and I let out a long sigh of relief. Television. Celeste mentioned something about it. Yet nothing could have quite prepared me.

I slowly wander the room, which is ablaze with blinking objects that seem somehow alive. A dark gray box underneath the television is marked with the letters VCR while beside it sits a lighter gray box that calls itself Super Nintendo. A sleek white desk holds an unusual sort of typewriter with a built-in screen. I venture toward it, pressing one of the keys, and then I jump back, startled, as the screen fills with the picture of an apple. "*Macintosh*," I whisper, reading the words below the image. What does that mean? The machine is now buzzing and whirring, and I back away from it.

Instead of artwork decorating the room, the walls are covered with huge color photographs. One depicts a scantily clad redheaded woman standing back-to-back with a gentleman, the words *Pretty Woman* running down the side of the image.

Another photograph shows five young men in matching jackets, with the phrase *Boyz II Men Cooleyhighharmony* written at the bottom.

I look around wildly, feeling dizzy at the sights and sounds within the room. I *don't belong in 1991*, I panic. *What am I doing?*

Just as I'm about to retreat, my father's face fills my mind. Father, who was powerful enough to travel through time even without his key, had believed me a worthy successor. Now is my chance to prove him right.

"I'll learn all I can about the 1990s right here. This room has all the knowledge I need," I tell myself. "And in a few days, my journey to the future will begin."

*Even if my memory were to fail me in the future, I would still be able to retrace, with certainty, the footsteps of my soul.* —YE SI

11

As Philip Walker drew closer to the Windsor Mansion on Sunday evening, it was with the sensation of returning to a place that had once meant a great deal to him. *What's happening to me?* He'd asked himself that question countless times since the day he'd arrived in New York, but he still had no clear answers, only pieces to a puzzle that he couldn't seem to solve.

Philip stood up straighter as he approached the tall entrance gates, his heartbeat picking up speed. The apartment building next door to the Windsor Mansion drew his attention, and as he glanced at it, his face paled. Somehow, he knew that building—just like he seemed to know the Windsor Mansion, without ever having stepped inside.

He shakily pressed the intercom button on the gate. A

woman's friendly voice answered and he cleared his throat before speaking.

"This is Philip Walker. I'm here to see Michele."

Michele knocked over her glass of water in surprise when Annaleigh informed her that Philip Walker was there. She hastily changed out of pajamas and threw on a pair of jeans and a cable-knit sweater, running a brush through her hair and dabbing on some lip gloss before hurrying down the stairs to meet him. The sight of Philip standing in the middle of the Grand Hall, ridiculously handsome in jeans and a black sweater, sent a buzz of electricity through her.

"Hi," she said, hoping her voice sounded a lot calmer than she felt.

"Hey. Sorry to just show up, I know it's late. I would have called, but I realized I don't have your number. Luckily your address is well-known." He grinned sheepishly.

"It's totally cool. What's up?" As she asked the question, Michele had a feeling she already knew the reason why he was there.

Philip glanced around uneasily then lowered his voice. "I . . . we need to talk about last night."

Michele spotted Annaleigh heading in their direction, and she gestured for Philip to follow her to the front door. "Want to go for a walk?"

"Sure."

He seemed to visibly relax at the idea of leaving the house, but his shoulders tensed when they stepped through the mansion gates, with Caissie's apartment building looming next door. Philip stared intently at it.

"It's funny—I could swear I know that place, but it looks all wrong. There was a house there, a mansion made of red brick and white stone. And I knew your house, too, before I ever went inside." He looked at Michele, and there was fear in his eyes. "Then last night, one minute we were talking in the lobby and everything was somewhat normal—and then it felt like I was this whole other person, this guy from another time and place who . . . who was crazy about you." A flush crept up Philip's cheeks.

All other thoughts were driven out of Michele's mind as she stared at him, amazement mingling with relief.

"You remember, then? You remember us at the dance together . . . in 1910?"

"I remember telling you the date was 1910," Philip said, in disbelief. "And I remember other things too—how it felt to miss you and wait for you. I felt how much he cared about you . . . like it was happening to me. And then this morning, I woke up earlier than usual. I was awake, but it was like I was sleepwalking." His voice sounded dazed as he recounted the story. "I felt older and heavier, like I wasn't seventeen anymore. I found myself at the piano, and then . . . I don't know how, but I started playing this song that I had never even *heard*. My mom came into the room while I was playing, and she said she knew the song. It's an old classical piece . . . called *Michele*."

Michele's throat was thick with tears.

"That piece was written by Phoenix Warren," she said

softly. "Whose real name was Philip Walker. He wrote that song for me . . . and then fifty years later, my mom named me after it."

Philip shook his head as if he weren't hearing correctly.

"And you're right," Michele continued. "There was a house here. It was the Walker Mansion, and you lived there a hundred years ago, decades before it was converted into this apartment building. And you *have* been inside my house, countless times. That's where we met."

Philip halted, staring at her. "What are you trying to say?"

"I'm saying that what the world considers impossible *is* possible—at least it is for us." She took a deep breath, a question suddenly occurring to her. "When's your birthday?"

"I'll be eighteen on December twelfth," he answered, giving her a quizzical look. "But I really don't understand—"

He broke off at Michele's expression.

"What is it?"

"He did it," Michele whispered. "Philip promised he'd find a way back to me. And he did."

"I am so completely lost here," Philip groaned.

"Just humor me. Do you know who else lived at the Osborne, later in his life?" Michele asked. "The same person who looks exactly like you, who played piano just the way you do. Phoenix Warren, aka Philip James Walker. And you were born on the *exact same day* that he died." Michele looked at Philip in awe. *Elizabeth was right.*

"It's almost as if his spirit left one body on December twelfth, 1992, and was . . . reborn in another," she continued. "Like reincarnation."

The color drained from Philip's face.

"This—this is getting even crazier than before," he stammered. "Me, the reincarnation of Phoenix Warren? What are you going to tell me next, that you were the real Billie Holiday and we were in a traveling music troupe together?"

Michele smiled grimly. "If you can believe it, the real story is maybe even more out there. Do you think you're ready to hear it?"

Philip took a deep breath. "As ready as I'll ever be."

They found themselves walking down Fifth Avenue, just as they had done the first time Michele confessed her true identity to him in 1910.

"I never knew my father, but when I moved to New York two months ago, I found something that belonged to him. It was a key. A special key . . . one that sends you back in time. I later found out that my dad was a time traveler from the nineteenth century who went into the future and fell in love with my mom. But he disappeared before he even knew she was pregnant."

Michele sucked in her breath as she realized she'd just told him her biggest secret. Now he knew the truth: that she was a freak of nature, a "time-crossed" daughter.

"Long story short, the key sent me back to the Windsor Mansion—in 1910. Only a couple people could see me while I was there, and Philip was one of them. We fell in love," she said quietly. "It was like something out of a movie, the type of relationship that I assumed was just a fantasy. But it was real for us. We even wrote music together. 'Bring The Colors Back' was our first song."

Philip swallowed hard, as a light seemed to dawn in his eyes.

"But our difference in Time was too big a hurdle," Michele continued, sadness creeping into her voice. "I couldn't control my time traveling, so sometimes he had to wait for weeks on end to see me, only to have me in 1910 for just a couple of hours. I couldn't exist fully in 1910, and I tried and failed to bring him into the twenty-first century with me. We couldn't go on like that, with a century between us. But even after, we never stopped loving each other. We exchanged letters when I traveled into the 1920s, and he left me a ring—the ring you're wearing right now."

Philip glanced down at his hand in shock. "This? My dad gave it to me. He said it was a family heirloom."

"Well, are you related to the same Walkers?" Michele asked with a faint smile.

Philip nodded. "I remember my dad telling me stories about visiting their Newport house as a kid, just before it was donated to the Preservation Society. It had a French-sounding name, Palais de la Mer or something."

"That's it!" Michele cried. "I was there. So then what your dad said was true. The ring is a family heirloom."

"But how would it get back into the family if your whole story is true and it was given to *you* all those years ago?" Philip challenged her.

"I don't know. But one of the last time periods I traveled to was 1944, and when I came back to the present, the ring was gone," Michele told him. "It was also in 1944 when I finally saw Philip again. This time he was all grown up, and he had changed his identity to Phoenix Warren. Faking the death of Philip Walker and taking on this new persona was the only way he could pursue his music and live in freedom from his oppressive mom and uncle. That was the night he told me he had written the symphony *Michele* for me."

Philip stared at her, speechless.

"That was the last time I saw him—before you showed up at school."

"So let me get this straight." Philip let out an incredulous laugh. "I'm supposed to believe that you're a time traveler and I'm a reincarnation of my great-great-great-uncle who also happens to be a famous musician who dated you a hundred years ago?"

Michele bit her lip. "Um. Yes. In a nutshell."

"Then either the world has gone insane, or we both have." Philip took a shaky breath. "I wish I could tell you no part of me identified with that unbelievable story you just told, but . . . well, I don't remember the events you mentioned, but it was weird—when you were talking, I felt like . . . like I knew what you were going to say before you said it. That déjà vu feeling." Philip was silent a moment. "*Home*—that's what I thought of when I saw you that first day in class. I felt like I'd come home again, and it confused the hell out of me. I've been feeling that way again since last night when we were—wherever that was— and I don't think I can fight it anymore."

He reached for her hand. As their fingers laced together, Michele felt a warm glow spreading through her, a happiness that she was almost afraid to trust.

"I've been so hopeful that you would remember—it's hard

to believe this moment is real," Michele blurted out. "How do I know you won't forget again, that things won't go back to the way they were before?"

"Because now that I've come out of this—this fog, I don't want to waste another second. I need to be in your life," he said firmly. "I can't stay away from you anymore."

His face was so sincere that Michele knew she could believe him. She didn't know who initiated it, but suddenly she found herself in his arms, her head nestled against his chest as he stroked her hair. Nothing had ever felt so perfect. *Philip is right,* she thought. *It does feel like coming home.*

"I can't believe this is real—that you're real," Michele murmured, closing her eyes.

"I know." Philip's breath was warm against her ear. "It's the funniest feeling—like I've found something I never knew I was missing."

Michele smiled, remembering when she met Philip for the first time in 1910. "I know just what you mean."

After what might have been minutes or hours in his embrace—she had lost all sense of time—Michele remembered her mission from the day before: to find out what Philip knew about Rebecca. She wished she could stretch this one moment of peace and never have to face the dawning threat, but she forced herself to speak up.

"I hate to bring this up now, but—about the other day in the choir room . . ." Her voice trailed off and Philip nodded for her to continue.

"When that woman—creature—showed up, it seemed like

you had seen her before," Michele said carefully. "I need to know, because—well—she wants to kill me."

Philip's face paled. *"What?"*

Michele began to tell him the story of Rebecca and her father, and the torment that had followed her family ever since. When she finished, Philip's response astonished her.

"You're going to think I'm crazy, but—I have a feeling I'm the one who is supposed to stop Rebecca."

*"You?"*

Philip's eyes took on the faraway, trancelike expression that Michele noticed whenever a memory of his former life took hold.

"Since I was a boy, I've had this recurring nightmare—her creepy voice in my ear, telling me there's a girl I have to stay away from. Once I moved to New York, she became more than just a voice. She started following me, haunting me with a new urgency—and now I could see her." He shuddered. "I think she *knows* that I can hurt her somehow. Or maybe the . . . the other Philip did something. That's why she didn't want me to find you—didn't want me to remember."

"I can't let you get in the middle of things with her," Michele insisted. "I already told Philip in the 1930s to stay away from her. I would never forgive myself if anything happened to you."

"It's too late for that," Philip said gently. "I'm already in the middle of it, and if I can somehow protect you, then I want to. We can't let Rebecca win."

Michele took a deep breath. She couldn't find the words to respond, but the look in his eyes let her know he understood.

A text alert sounded on her phone, jolting Michele out of the moment. She glanced down to read the message from Annaleigh: *So sorry to interrupt! But your grandparents said it's getting late and they're anxious for you to come home.*

"I should get back," Michele said reluctantly.

"Okay, I'll walk you home."

Michele felt a glimmer of delight at the disappointed look on Philip's face. *He wants to spend more time with me!* she thought happily. Once they reached Windsor Mansion, there was a nervous pause before they said goodbye, until Philip gave her a soft kiss on the cheek. "See you tomorrow."

"Good night," she called, her cheek tingling from his kiss. She stayed in the Grand Hall for a few minutes after Philip left, feeling a ridiculous urge to break into a happy dance.

## DAY SIX

*Michele Windsor sat on a rickety rocking chair in the drawing room of a brownstone townhouse. A thin novel lay across her lap, but she ignored the words waiting on its pages. Glancing out the window of the sparsely decorated room, she sighed heavily at the sight of Gramercy Park below her, looking like a sibling of the park she had known in her youth—in the other Time. It was similar in appearance but different in personality; its greenery and shrubbery shinier, newer. Gazing at the park was yet another sign that Michele didn't belong here.*

*She watched the scene below her window: rough-hewn women hawking flowers and fruit outside the gates, while the upper-middle-class ladies inside chatted genially on pristine benches, ig-*

noring their poorer sisters outside the park. Gentlemen in top hats and walking suits paced the lawn, cigars dangling from their lips as they spoke, their sober expressions suggesting the topic of conversation was business. Children ran through the grass, shouting and playing, while harried nannies trailed after them.

Michele watched the park every day, waiting, numbly biding her time until her entrapment in 1904 ended. She couldn't remember how long she'd been stuck here, in limbo, unable to reach Philip or her father . . . or anyone she knew.

Her scalp ached and she reached up, desperate to topple the tightly wound ringlets piled on her head, but she stopped herself just in time. She knew it would only be more of a bother to have to reconstruct the elaborate hairstyle again later. She fiddled with the tall collar of her afternoon dress, which always seemed to make her neck feel itchy, while the corset that slimmed her waist caused her breath to come out in shallow gasps. Michele thought longingly of her girlhood, when she dressed in free, unrestricted clothing. It felt so long ago that she could hardly envision what those clothes looked like, but she remembered how light she had once felt, running through the city in cotton fabrics, with none of these heavy skirts weighing her down.

"You're trapped here, aren't you?"

Her head snapped up. She knew who was speaking before she even saw her face. Rebecca Windsor, her dark vicious eyes glaring at her in the dull light of the room.

"I tried to warn your foolish grandparents of this. A time-crossed child is an aberration. And nature always corrects its mistakes." Rebecca stalked forward. That was when Michele saw the knife glittering in her pocket. She opened her mouth to scream *as Rebecca raised the blade, but no sound came out. Everything turned black.*

Michele woke from the nightmare in a cold sweat, gasping for air. As the sight of her bedroom filled her vision, her heartbeat slowly returned to normal. She exhaled shakily, relief flooding through her as she looked around and saw that she was, without a doubt, in her true Time. *That was just a dream, but this is reality. I'm here, where I'm supposed to be.* Yet she couldn't help wondering if it was a warning. She shuddered, remembering what it had felt like to be prisoner of another Time. All the thrills of time travel had disappeared when she was trapped, leaving only the desperate sensation of a lost child trying to get back home.

She found Walter and Dorothy sitting together in the Grand Hall, making a pretense of conversation, but Michele knew they had been waiting to catch her before school. With the seventh day approaching, she could see the growing anxiety in their faces. "Stay home today," Dorothy blurted out. "We'd feel better."

"You don't have to worry about me leaving the house. It's not like Rebecca is any less dangerous here," Michele pointed out.

"But *we're* here," Dorothy insisted.

Michele squeezed her grandmother's hand. "I promise I'm being careful. It almost seems safer to go on with my normal life—like it'll be harder for her to get to me when I'm surrounded by people, as opposed to the three of us sitting at home waiting."

Walter nodded. "Come home straight after school, then."

"I have an appointment with Elizabeth," she told him. "But I promise to come home right after that."

Philip was standing by her locker when Michele arrived at school, and the sight was enough to temporarily drive away all her fear. He looked like a vision straight out of her daydreams, from the quiet happiness in his smile when he saw her approach to the way he leaned against her locker as if telling the world he was waiting for her. But the most fantastical part of all was that he finally belonged in her own Time. He was back—*they* were back—and the miracle of it seemed powerful enough to keep them safe, no matter the danger.

"Hi," she greeted him, unable to control her growing smile. He grinned back at her. At first the two of them hesitated, unsure what to do, but then he pulled her into his arms, wrapping her in a hug. Though it was quick, Michele felt the lingering closeness of his embrace even after they pulled away.

She heard a slight gasp behind her, and she and Philip both looked up to see Kaya Morgan push past them, her eyes red.

"What happened?" Michele asked in a low voice.

"I ended it," he said, looking after Kaya awkwardly. "I went to her place this morning and had the conversation. Not that there was much to end. She's a great person, but we were just hanging out. It wasn't anything serious. I liked her mostly because she distracted me."

"From what?"

"From you," Philip confessed. "From the way I felt whenever I saw you."

"Was it so bad?" Michele asked, only half kidding.

"I felt like I'd lost my mind around you," Philip said quietly. "I still feel that way. Looking at you, I get these—these flashes of memory, and the only thing that makes me feel better is when . . ." He broke off, and reached for her hand. Michele felt her heart jump at his touch.

The bell rang, and Michele and Philip glanced down, smiling nervously as they walked hand-in-hand toward U.S. history. Michele felt like they were under a spotlight as students in the halls openly gawked at them. They passed by Olivia and her snobbish group of Old New York descendants, who immediately began stage-whispering about "the shocking alliance of a Windsor and a Walker!" while a trio of freshmen stopped in their tracks to stare.

Michele and Philip dropped their hands when they reached the classroom, but it was clear that everyone inside had already seen. Ben stared down at his desk while Kaya gave Philip a pained look. Michele lowered her eyes guiltily, wishing there was a way she and Philip could be happy without anyone else having to get hurt. She scanned the room for Caissie, knowing that at least one person would be glad to see them together—but she wasn't there.

When the bell rang for lunch, Michele practically flew to the dining room. The few hours alone had left her practically delirious with the need to see Philip, to feel his closeness. She wondered if their separation had given her a new, deeper urgency in her feelings toward him. Knowing what it felt like to lose him, even though she now had him back, left a lingering pain, like a scar that still stung.

Her anxiety lightened when she saw Philip standing in the lunch line, looking her way. She grinned and caught up to him.

"Hey," he greeted her with a smile.

"Hi." Michele heard grumbling behind her.

"I probably shouldn't be cutting in line," she said sheepishly. "I'm going to go to the back, but do you—do you want to sit at our table?"

"Yeah," he replied warmly. "I'll get your lunch, don't worry about waiting in line."

"You sure?" Michele looked up at him, her cheeks flushed. She wondered if this counted as their first official date in the twenty-first century.

"Of course I'm sure. I'll come find you at your table," he told her. "What can I get you?"

"Oh . . . I'll have the pasta and an iced tea," she told him shyly. "Thanks."

Michele skipped toward her usual table, to find only Aaron sitting down.

"Hey, Aaron. Do you know where Caissie is?"

"No idea."

Michele narrowed her eyes. "Wait—have you guys talked since the dance?"

"Not exactly," Aaron said uncomfortably. "Things have been so weird since then. We probably shouldn't have gone together."

"Why do you say that? Is it because of the sophomore girl you were dancing with? Are you really into her?" Michele asked, disappointed. She'd been rooting for Caissie and Aaron to get together, ever since becoming friends with the two of them.

"No! But she's been acting so cold to me over that, when she's the one who was with that Willis dude half the night."

"It's only because she was hurt," Michele told him. "You kind of blew her off."

"I didn't! I just—I don't know." Aaron glanced down at his plate. "It felt strange, being on a date with her."

"In a good or bad way?"

"Good," Aaron admitted. "But still weird. She's been my friend forever."

"I really think you guys just need to talk. You're too good together to let anything get in the way," Michele encouraged him.

Aaron diverted the subject as he spotted Philip heading toward their table. "So the rumors are true," he said under his breath. "I'm impressed. No one's ever taken a guy away from Kaya Morgan before." He reached up to high-five Michele, but she ignored him.

"I didn't *take* him from anyone. It was just . . . we're supposed to be together."

"Uh, *o*-kay," Aaron laughed.

Ignoring all the eyes in the dining room focused their way, Philip placed the two lunch trays onto the table and took the seat next to Michele. She smiled at him. As the three of them talked easily, Michele felt the urge to pinch herself to prove that he was actually here—and that this happiness was real.

After school, Michele stepped out of the Windsors' SUV and in front of the Dorilton on West Seventy-First Street. For a moment she just stood outside, looking at the Beaux-Arts limestone and brick castle of an apartment building. With its massive sculptures, arched balconies, and towering mansard roof, the Dorilton reminded Michele of something out of a Walt Disney fairy tale—except there was nothing childlike or innocent about it. The building looked as if it had stood on New York soil forever, with decades of secrets buried in its walls.

After Elizabeth buzzed her in, the iron gates swung open and Michele walked up to the main entrance and into the formal lobby. Taking the elevator up to the tenth floor, she followed a long hallway until she reached Elizabeth's apartment.

"So good to see you again!" Elizabeth hugged her warmly, and Michele again felt the instantaneous ease of being in her presence. She followed Elizabeth into the spacious, whimsically decorated apartment, until they reached a New Age-y meditation room. The walls were decorated with colored scarves, and a soft blue chaise stood in the center, surrounded by cozy floor cushions. Crystals hung from the windows, creating rainbows in the room as they caught the light, while burning incense and essential oils filled the space with a soothing scent.

"Go ahead and lie down on the chaise," Elizabeth instructed Michele. "Today we'll be following my methodology of using deep breathing and relaxation to awaken the subconscious. Close your eyes and concentrate on your breathing. Simply breathe in . . . and out . . . in . . . and out . . ."

Michele followed the breathing pattern, Elizabeth's melodic voice lulling her into a state of hypnosis. Michele's eyes were closed as if she were sleeping, yet they moved furtively beneath her shut eyelids.

"Now see yourself standing in a big circular room. As you look around, you see that you are standing before a mirror. You watch as the image in the mirror becomes clearer," Elizabeth instructed. "You touch your face and the image mimics your movement. And you realize that this image is you, as you are now in this lifetime—but you are in the distant past."

Even in her state of hypnosis, Michele recognized that the girl in the mirror looked *just like* her dream from the night before—the Michele who was trapped in 1904. Her hair was dressed in a poufy pompadour topped off with an elaborate picture hat, and she wore a starched white blouse tucked into a floor-length slate-blue skirt. As Michele looked in the mirror, her fear slipped away. She knew it was time to find her father.

Letting her mind focus on the desired Time like an incantation, Michele felt the air swirl around her body, and her stomach jumped as she rose above the floor. She slowly blinked her eyes open, knowing that everything she was about to see would be different.

Elizabeth and the meditation room had disappeared. In fact, *everything* in the room was gone. Michele stood in the middle of an abandoned apartment, with nothing surrounding her but cherrywood floors and bare walls. It was completely silent until she heard the *swish* of ice skates, and Michele hurried to the window, catching her breath at the sight.

New York was blanketed in snow. The rolling hills of Central Park were a glistening white, while the trees glittered with flurries instead of leaves. Spread out below the Dorilton was a small pond of ice, with two smiling young boys dressed in winter leggings, wool coats, and fur hats skating along its surface. At the edge of the rink, Michele spotted a liveried footman helping a lady shrouded in a heavy velvet coat exit a horse-drawn carriage.

*I did it. I went back in time—without the key!* Did that mean she, Michele Windsor, was one of the Timekeepers with this rare ability? Or was this all a byproduct of hypnosis?

Michele stepped out of the empty apartment and raced through the corridor into the elevator, her eyes widening as she reached the lobby and main entrance of the Dorilton. A line of carriages bordered the porte cochere, and displays of turn-of-the-century winter fashions adorned the men and women who swarmed the entrance, from voluminous coats and veils on the ladies to fur-collar overcoats and homburg hats on the gentlemen. Though fascinated by the wintry Old New York scene, Michele shifted her focus to the Windsor Mansion. She remembered Walter's words, that in the 1900s Irving was not just the family lawyer but also a close friend, and she knew home was the first place to begin her search.

Using nothing more than the power of her mind, Michele directed her thoughts to the Windsor Mansion of 1904. With a jolt, she was lifted off the snow, her body sent spinning, until she landed with a stumble on familiar ground.

As she stood outside the entrance gates, the Walker Mansion pulled her gaze. Philip was likely somewhere inside; only he would be just twelve years old in 1904, far too young to know her. Michele glanced up at the house that would one day be a modern apartment building and saw a shocking flash of yellow—a familiar ponytail darting past the front window. The figure hurried out the door, bounding down the steps in jeans and a trench coat.

Michele watched, stunned, as the girl strode toward Windsor Mansion. Her expression was alight with awe as she took in the surroundings of 1904, oblivious to who was waiting for her. Michele could practically hear her heart thudding through her chest as she followed the blond ponytail, the distance between them growing smaller until they were both at the same streetlamp covered in snow at the end of the block.

"Caissie."

She jumped at the sound of Michele's voice. Slowly, she turned around.

"It *is* you," Michele whispered in horror.

Caissie's eyes filled with panic as she looked at Michele. Before Michele could say another word Caissie took off, sprinting away from her toward the hotel next door. Still in shock, Michele needed a few moments to register what had happened. Her legs felt weak as she ran after Caissie, hurrying up the stairs to an unfamiliar Renaissance building that bore the name PLAZA HOTEL. Her mind numbly registered that this must be the first Plaza, the short-lived hotel that was later rebuilt into a landmark.

Michele pushed through the front doors of the old Plaza, adrenaline surging through her as she scanned the lobby. She saw a blur of furs and mufflers as guests socialized before the fire, but no sign of Caissie. Michele turned around just in time to spot the blond ponytail disappearing out the Plaza doors. She raced after Caissie. As her feet hit the curb outside the

Plaza, she felt a scream rise in her throat, and she clapped her hand over her mouth to stop it.

A sinister, dark-haired woman was just feet away from Michele, marching purposefully toward the Windsor Mansion. She stared straight ahead with steely eyes, unaware of Michele's presence.

*It's Rebecca—in her own Time,* Michele realized with horror. She was older now, in her thirties, and her face had a pinched and puckered expression, as if permanently repulsed. Rebecca pulled a stopwatch from the pocket of her floor-length skirt and then quickened her pace toward the Windsor Mansion. Michele hung back, her palms clammy with fear as she hid in the shadows of the Plaza's awning.

As soon as Rebecca disappeared from view, Michele sped across the street, darting between two horse-drawn carriages, her eyes searching frantically for Caissie. Her heart leaped into her throat when she finally saw Caissie running toward Central Park. Michele took a deep breath and sprinted through the oncoming traffic, her feet throbbing as she ran, until she reached the Artists Gate entrance to the park. At last she caught up to Caissie. Michele took her by surprise, yanking her ponytail, and Caissie fell backward.

"OW!"

Without missing a beat, Michele snatched her key from around Caissie's neck and grabbed onto Caissie with her other hand.

"Windsor Mansion, present-day!" she cried into the air.

Caissie screamed bloody murder as their bodies rose and spun through the air. When they landed on the ground in front of the Windsor Mansion gates, she leaned over to retch in the bushes, causing a passing couple to exclaim with disgust. Michele ignored them, relief filling her lungs as she fastened the key around her neck. There was hope again. But when she turned back to Caissie, shock and anger flooded her anew.

"What the hell is going on?" she demanded.

"H-how did you do it?" Caissie's voice was a terrified squeak. "How did you get there?"

"You mean without my key that you *stole*?" Michele's voice rose as she stared at her friend in dismay. It was Irving and Rebecca's story all over again. "I trusted you, I confided in you! How could you do that to me?"

"It's not—it's not what you think," Caissie stammered. "I didn't know what I was doing."

"Oh, right, because it's *so* easy to just accidentally steal a necklace," Michele scoffed.

"That's not what I mean." Caissie took a shaky breath. "It was . . . this *voice* I heard. When the blackout happened, I was passing the choir room on my way to class and I kept hearing someone calling to me—telling me I had to take your key, that it wasn't just for my benefit but yours too."

Michele looked at her in disbelief. "You actually expect me to buy this?"

"I couldn't see anyone, but the voice kept telling me that you were in trouble—that you weren't supposed to time travel anymore, that you're *time-crossed* and if I wanted you to stay alive, I had to take your key away—and bring it here."

Michele froze at the words *time-crossed*. She had definitely never told Caissie anything about that.

"Did you see the person whose voice you heard?" Michele asked urgently. *Did Caissie have the Gift of Sight?*

"No, I couldn't see anyone or anything," Caissie admitted. "It was just a woman's voice—but I swear, I'm telling the truth. She told me to bring the key to the Windsor Mansion in 1904, that she'd be waiting for me there—waiting to help us both."

Michele drew in a sharp breath.

"That person is trying to kill me. So unless you're on her side, which maybe you are, I suggest you stop listening to voices."

Caissie's jaw dropped. "I—you never told me—I didn't realize . . ." Tears sprang to her eyes. "I'm really sorry."

"Was that the real reason you stole my key and pretended like you knew nothing about it when I told you it was missing?" Michele asked evenly.

Caissie's face crumpled. "Okay, I'll admit that I wanted to see the past. I mean, it wasn't *fair* that you were the one who got to have all these adventures, and I had to be the lowly sidekick just hearing about it all! When I thought that I could experience time travel too, and help you in the process . . . it just seemed too good not to try. I never meant to hurt you. And besides, it turns out you don't even need the key! What's that about?" Caissie looked at her in amazement.

"I don't know *what's* going on. If you had any idea how crazy my life has been . . ." Michele's voice trailed off. "I don't know what to believe anymore. Maybe you didn't mean to hurt me, but the fact that you would lie like that and steal from me . . . that changes things. I don't know how I can trust you anymore."

Caissie looked away. "I get it." She bit her lip. "I'm so sorry. I hope you can forgive me."

Michele nodded but didn't speak. Caissie lingered a moment, then got to her feet.

"I should go home," she mumbled. "I'll see you at school."

Michele watched Caissie walk away, a knot forming in her stomach. If Rebecca could convince her own friend to turn on her, then things were even more dire than she'd thought. And if Michele hadn't seen Rebecca in the nick of time, she would have walked straight into Rebecca's clutches. Michele had encroached on Rebecca's own Timeline by entering a year where she lived and possessed her full strength and power—a Time when Rebecca had no need to wait seven days.

Rebecca had somehow known that 1904 was where Michele would go.

There have only been a few Timekeepers to possess the ability to travel without their Key. Those of us with this rare skill experience a stronger presence when time traveling, and may find additional powers within as the years pass. Like petals opening on a budding flower, we too seem to be constantly in bloom.

—THE HANDBOOK OF THE TIME SOCIETY

Michele returned to Elizabeth's apartment in a state of fluster.

"How did that *happen*?" she exclaimed as soon as Elizabeth opened the door. "Did I just disappear into thin air from your meditation room? And was it all from hypnosis, or did I actually travel through time without a key?"

Elizabeth was beaming with pride. It was clear she'd been hoping for this result when she set up the day's session.

"You did disappear from the room, though I wasn't worried. I knew you were still here—just in a different year," she said simply. "And I believe it was a combination of hypnosis with your innate time-travel abilities that caused it. In fact, have you ever noticed brief moments when you feel as if you've slipped into a different time—without intending to or realizing it?"

Michele nodded, remembering the dance with Philip and when she ran to the Osborne while watching time change around her.

"You see, you were so conditioned to believe that you could only travel with the key, you needed a little help from your subconscious to show that *you* are the one with the power," Elizabeth explained. "You have a true gift, Michele—unlike anything I've seen before."

Michele sank into a chair in amazement. "I—I don't know what to say! All along I thought I was just lucky to have found my dad's key, and of course I still think that, but now to know it's my own ability too, is an incredible feeling. Thank you for showing me."

"Thank *you* for letting me witness something so extraordinary," Elizabeth returned earnestly.

Michele noticed the hour on the overhead clock and stood up. "My grandparents want me home on the early side, but before I go, there's somewhere in particular that I need to travel to. Do you mind if I make the jump from here?"

Elizabeth grinned. "Go for it."

And so Michele closed her eyes, focusing on the headquarters of the Time Society . . . where she hoped to find the remaining answers she needed.

"And *who* might you be?"

Michele's eyes fluttered open at the sound of a man's surprised voice. She felt herself sinking into a carpeted floor as she gripped the key necklace.

"Ahem." The voice was back in her ear again. "Care to tell me who you are? I know you're not registered, so how on earth did you get into the Aura?"

*The Aura.* Michele sucked in her breath at the realization that she had made it—that she was finally in the place she had read and wondered so much about. She looked around at the cavernous, dark-wood lobby and her mouth fell open at the sight of all the people.

A couple sat together by the fireplace, the man dressed in a three-piece striped suit and 1920s-style Panama hat, while the woman wore a sleeveless black mod dress reminiscent of Audrey Hepburn. Through the lobby's double doors burst a young man dressed in a silver uniform made from a fabric Michele couldn't identify. He spoke into a device that looked like a cell phone, and a hologram of a smiling woman appeared beside him. Michele shook her head in amazement. These people were fascinating. *Timekeepers.* Each of them from a different era.

Coming out of her daze, Michele realized that the voice she had heard was speaking to her. She turned around to find herself slumped in front of a long reception desk, while a middle-aged man wearing spectacles and a nametag that read "Victor" stood, peering down at her.

"Sorry, I'm a little out of it," she told him apologetically. "I'm Michele."

Victor glanced down at the key around her neck, and his spine stiffened. "And what would your last name be?"

"Windsor."

Victor immediately picked up his phone. "Ida. Michele Windsor has arrived."

Michele eyed Victor suspiciously. The way he had spoken, it sounded like this Ida person had been expecting her.

"Follow me." Victor slipped out from behind the reception desk.

"Where are we going?" Michele asked. "Who's Ida?"

"Who's Ida?" Victor repeated, in apparent disbelief at such a question. "Only the president of the Time Society!"

"What about Millicent?"

Victor looked at her sharply. "How do you know about Millicent?"

Michele bit her lip. There was no simple answer to that question. "I . . . I read about her."

She followed Victor through the winding corridors until they reached a tall bronze doorframe.

"Come in," a clear, bright voice called from behind it.

As Michele entered, she realized that this must have been Millicent's drawing room, the setting of Irving's confrontation with Rebecca. It looked just like his description.

Ida stood up, a mercurial figure with catlike gray eyes and short, curly dark hair. She was dressed in what looked like a business suit of the 1950s, a short-sleeved powder-blue jacket with a peplum and a full skirt. Her face had the otherworldly look of someone far older than her generation, but without the lines and wrinkles that characterized the elderly.

"Thank you, Victor." As he left the room, Ida's focus turned to Michele, fixing her with a scrutinizing glance.

"Hello, Michele. Please have a seat. I always wondered when you would find us. Your story is one I know so well."

"What do you mean?" Michele pressed.

"I met your father once," she said, her expression far-off. "I wasn't born until 1920, but I joined the Society in my teens and quickly rose through the ranks working for them." She gestured to her presidential surroundings, as if proving her point. "One of my assignments—missions, we call them at the Society—when I was twenty years old, was to go back in time to February the second, 1888. Strange things had happened that day, and I was instructed to be another witness to the events.

"Another Timekeeper, Hiram King, and I were to lead a girl named Rebecca Windsor around the Headquarters and show her to then-president Millicent August's office, as if she were joining the Society," Ida recollected. "But it was all a set-up. When Hiram and I brought Rebecca into this very room, Millicent and your father were waiting to confront her, to take back the key and the power that she had stolen from Irving. She was banned from the premises and escorted back to New York, while Irving Henry became our newest member. It was a day none of us could forget. It was the first and only time we have ever had an impostor attempt to infiltrate our world."

Ida paused for a moment, as if seeing that day all over again in her mind. She continued, "After Irving was inducted into the Society, he decided to stay here at the Aura for a while, and he chose the year 1991 for his first mission. All of our rooms are decorated and furnished in the style of the date that denotes them, and we also provide documents and literature on the era in each guestroom. So after spending a few days immersing himself in 1991, he disappeared into the future.

"One of the young Timekeepers who helped prepare Irving

209

went upstairs to check on him and found his room empty. We were all pleased for him, knowing this meant he must have made a successful trip into the future. But that was the last our Society ever saw of Irving Henry. He was thought to have so much potential, especially with his father having been one of Millicent's favorites—but he never set foot near Society Headquarters again.

"Rumors floated back and forth, but no one knew the truth about Irving's disappearance—not until the Windsors' Halloween Ball of 1910. That was the night when you were seen dancing with Philip Walker, by the very Timekeeper who had become friends with Irving all those years ago, the girl who helped prepare him for the 1990s. She spotted your resemblance to Irving right away, but more importantly, she recognized the key. The fact that most of the guests couldn't see you further proved that you were his daughter—a time traveler."

Michele stared at Ida, stunned. The night of the Ball, she'd been so certain that only Clara and Philip had seen her. The knowledge that she had been watched the whole time, her actions reported on, left her speechless.

"A little digging was all it took to confirm what we had suspected: That you are not a natural child, but a child born across times. By remaining in the 1990s for so long and conceiving a child, your father broke two of our greatest laws," Ida said frankly. "And that's not the worst of it. One week after the Halloween Ball, Millicent August was found dead—her key stolen. Her great-niece, who was supposed to inherit Millicent's place in the Society, never got the chance."

Michele covered her mouth with her hands, sickened by the story. "Who would do something so evil?"

Ida looked her straight in the eye. "Rebecca. Her fingerprints were recorded when she first entered the Aura back in 1888, and those same prints were found on Millicent's clothes the night of the murder. Two different witnesses saw a figure matching Rebecca's description enter and exit Millicent's house that fatal evening. There is no doubt: Rebecca killed Millicent. And now she can travel through time, she can Age Shift and thereby exist beyond her death—all because she has Millicent's key."

Michele gripped the sides of her chair, her stomach churning. "And now she's after me. She's been haunting me, trying to hurt me—and I can't understand why."

"It's because you represent everything that, in Rebecca's mind, was taken from her," Ida explained. "She feels that your power, your key, all should have been hers instead, and would have been had she not gotten caught in her scheme. Moreover, you represent her heartbreak. The idea that Irving found love with someone else in her own family, and actually went on to have a child—it drove her mad. For some people, especially the entitled, disappointment can be the most dangerous of emotions." Ida took a deep breath. "Rebecca found out about you the same way we all did, at the Windsors' Halloween Ball. The one honest gift she ever had was the Gift of Sight, and she saw you too."

"She was *there*?" Michele fought back the bile rising in her throat. "Why—why can't someone just rip the key off her neck? She's powerless without it."

"It's not that simple," Ida said grimly. "She knows to stay away from the Society, so we have to find *her*—and that's nearly impossible when she is no longer a living human being, but an Age Shifting spirit who can disappear at will. Death coupled with the power of Millicent's key has made Rebecca nearly invincible."

Michele's head was spinning. "Wait . . . what do you mean, she's an Age Shifting spirit?"

"Age Shifting is the ability to travel through time in the body of your older or younger self. So let's say a Timekeeper the same age as Rebecca, a woman of thirty-nine in 1910, has a mission taking her to your time, 2010. But for the purposes of the mission, she needs to appear seventeen in your era. The thirty-nine-year-old would first travel back in time to when *she* was seventeen, in 1888, and must come face to face with her younger self. One person cannot physically exist in two different bodies in the same Time and place. So when the older Timekeeper grabs hold of her seventeen-year-old self, the two merge into one body. Now she is physically seventeen, but still nearly forty in mind and maturity. This ability is one of the great temptations of time travel," Ida revealed. "The power to be young without having to relearn the lessons of youth. Larger than that, however, is the idea that through Age Shifting time travel, a Timekeeper who technically died in the twentieth century could appear in your twenty-first century as a young adult. This is what we mean by Rebecca existing beyond her death."

"And can she stay that way indefinitely?" Michele asked, aghast. "How am I ever supposed to get rid of her if that's the case?"

"No one can Age Shift forever," Ida clarified. "It takes a tremendous toll on the body. We are particularly able to control it in the Society through our law that forbids Timekeepers from staying in another time past the Seven Days. Before reaching Visibility, Age Shifting can only last for hours at a time—then you are returned to the body you came from, the body of your true age. However, those who break the law and stay in another Time past the Seven Days can maintain their Age Shifting identity for much longer. Though again, it can never be permanent."

Michele swallowed hard, her throat suddenly dry.

"Tomorrow will mark the seventh day that she's been in my time. So tomorrow she will be strong enough to—to kill me . . . right?"

"She's staying the full seven days?" Ida's face turned ashen. "Yes. Before time travelers reach Visibility, they are inhibited from affecting life. They cannot kill, nor can they conceive. But after the Seven Days have been attained . . . I'm afraid there's nothing you can do but fight. Because of the laws your father broke, the two of you are not legitimate members of the Society, so I'm afraid we cannot offer you protection. But what you can do is use your key to outsmart her, by concealing yourself in different Times."

"But I don't want to live in hiding," Michele said in frustration. "I want to *end* this, not continue to be at Rebecca's mercy. Please . . . isn't there *anything* I can do?"

Ida hesitated.

"Millicent had a theory," she began. "She had the idea that Age Shifting Timekeepers could only cease to exist if they were killed in multiple Timelines besides their own. Of course, this was never proven, and I imagine it would be incredibly difficult to accomplish. But Millicent believed in her theory with conviction." Ida looked at her carefully. "I don't know that I would advise attempting it under any circumstances, but certainly not alone."

The clock sounded and Ida stood up, signaling the end of their meeting.

"Wait!" Michele called out. "There's one more thing I need to know. What's so bad about being born to parents from two different times? Why is it against the law? What's going to happen to me?"

Ida hesitated before answering. "It's against nature, against the rules of Time, for a child to live and grow up in one century when one of her parents is from another. Let me ask, have you ever found yourself time traveling against your will? Have you been pushed back to the present when you hoped to remain in the past, or vice versa?"

"Yes," Michele admitted. "It's happened a number of times."

"That is your body's gravity, trying to pull you back into the past where half of you belongs. We've seen this with a few other time-crossed children. Gradually, usually beginning around adulthood, they become split between their father's and mother's time periods, involuntarily pulled from one era to another." Ida looked at her sadly. "That means that you might be having the best day of your life here in the twenty-first century, only to be propelled back one hundred years before, for who knows how long. It's enough to drive you mad—and it makes having a normal life an impossible task."

Michele shook her head frantically. "No. No, that won't happen to me! I *can't* be a prisoner of Time like that. There's got to be an exception. *I've* got to be the exception. I can't get stuck in the past, not now that I've found—" She broke off midsentence, not ready to talk about Philip just yet.

"Millicent used to say there is a way around every hurdle," Ida shared. "In this case . . . you'll have to be the one to discover it."

"What is it about 1904?" Michele asked. "The times that I've recently gone into the past involuntarily, it's been to 1904."

"You're sixteen years old, aren't you?" When Michele nodded Ida continued, "Your father came to the future from early 1888. Had you been born in your father's time, you would be sixteen years old in 1904. So the split is already taking place. You have two Timelines now, one as a sixteen-year-old girl in the twenty-first century . . . and the other as a sixteen-year-old of 1904."

The color drained from Michele's face.

"What if—what if I can travel without a key?" she asked, grasping for straws. "What then?"

Ida's movements stilled, and she looked at Michele in astonishment. "That I would very much like to see."

Who do I belong to,
Who belongs to me in this life?
There exist no love songs,
Tender is the key of my strife.
I'll fill the world with my creations,
Live the soul of imagination.
Who do I belong to,
Who belongs to me?
When I look inside me, who will I meet?
Leave the past and present behind me,
Let the future steer and guide me.
Who do I belong to?
The one who left the key.
Now it's time for me
To be who he thought I could be.

—IRVING HENRY
FEBRUARY 5, 1991

## THE DIARY OF IRVING HENRY
### *February* 5, 1888

"I am ready," I whisper to the key in my hand. "Take me to New York City, in the year 1991."

I cry out, currents of shock coursing through me as invisible strings pull my body above the floor. I rise like a phantom over Room 1991, higher and higher, until I am nearing the colossal ceiling of the Aura Hotel. And then my body begins to spin faster than I've ever imagined possible, so fast that I find myself clawing at the air in a desperate attempt to slow down. I feel violently ill, like my heart might give out on me at any moment. It isn't *human* to move at such a speed!

Shooting through the roof of the Aura, I yell in terror as I find myself soaring into the open air, the sand and beaches of San Diego so far below that they look like tiny dots of color.

I'm *flying*! Adrenaline mixes with dread as I realize there is no one to catch my fall. Suddenly, the scene around me swiftly begins changing. Instead of a beach down at ground level, I see what looks like an island—an island containing the grid of a city. And then I spot something vaguely familiar, shining a light and beckoning me from below. A small copper structure standing on a pedestal—a statue that, as my body begins involuntarily hurtling downward, reveals itself to be the shape of a woman. She wears a spiked crown and proudly waves a torch into the air. It is the new gift from France.

*Lady Liberty.*

My face stretches into a smile as my fear leaves me. The Statue of Liberty is welcoming me back—back to New York, but into the future—and I whoop, waving my arms like a bird as I soar closer and closer to the ground.

"So I'm all, *'Talk to the hand, and don't even think about calling me after pulling that shadiness!'* I went postal on him."

"*You tell him, chica!*"

"*Jake, stop pushing your sister or I'm taking your Game Boy for the rest of the trip.*"

"*No fair, Mom, she started it!*"

"All right, stop, collaborate and listen/Ice is back with my brand-new invention—"

"*Dude, turn down the Walkman.*"

I kneel on the floor of Grand Central Terminal, my head in my hands as I fight the motion sickness threatening to overcome me. I'm too weak to open my eyes, but I hear a cacophony of voices and foreign sounds all around me—the voices of the 1990s. *I made it!*

When I finally look up, I hastily lean back against the wall to keep from falling over in shock.

Spending the past few days at the Aura Hotel, studying and learning all about the 1990s, could never have fully prepared me for actually being here, among the real, living, breathing humans of the future.

The ladies hurry toward the train platforms dressed in what looks like men's clothing: high-waisted, pale blue jeans, wide-leg black trousers, and baggy black knickers over black stockings. Some wear oversized denim shirts, while others have on high-collared sweaters that Celeste called "turtlenecks." Their heavy winter coats are missing all the flounces and frills of my day, while their hair, too, couldn't be more different from what I'm accustomed to. I see ladies with poufy, wavy hair worn down to their backs; others with shorter, straighter locks that fringe across their foreheads; and half a dozen actually sport a man's cropped haircut!

The young men are dressed similarly to my costume, though where my T-shirt and jeans look stiffly brand-new, their clothing appears lived-in and comfortable. Some of the boys my age even flaunt long, greasy hair and visible tears in their jeans, as if they're *trying* to look bedraggled. However, I spot a few middle-aged men who look more like my Victorian peers, buttoned up in wool coats over sweater-vests, long-sleeved shirts and gray trousers. The more casual gentlemen wear jeans with plaid shirts and suspenders.

The children running and playing throughout the station mark one of the most significant changes between my time and the 1990s. While Victorian children always dress formally for travel and are expected to follow their parents with utter deference, these rambunctious youngsters look like *they* are the ones controlling the parents, and their clothing seems more suited for playing outside than taking a trip on the train. Boys and girls alike wear jeans and farmer-like overalls with colorful jackets and sneakers.

I blink rapidly as I watch the scene in front of me. I'm so astonished by the people, it takes me several minutes before I discover that I am viewing a completely new Grand Central. The L-shaped depot has been replaced by a breathtaking building with floor-to-ceiling windows, marble staircases that lead to restaurants on indoor balconies, and a domed ceiling studded with stars.

I gingerly step forward into the rush of traffic and smile as the crowds throng around me, no one noticing my presence— yet I am truly among them! It's incredible, and suddenly I find myself picking up my pace, running to the nearest door. I have to see New York.

The sounds, smells, and sights of a new city seem to swallow me whole as I push through the doors and out onto Forty-Second Street. I gaze in openmouthed amazement at this foreign New York. It seems to have grown *vertically* over the past hundred years, as towering buildings stretch into the sky and loom over the sidewalks. Gone are all the horse-drawn carriages, landaus, and broughams trotting down the cobblestone streets, replaced instead with horseless automobiles and yellow cabs that zoom over paved roads. No Elevated Railroad chugs overhead, but a strange sound whirs from above. I cover my head in shock, as I look up to find *flying machines* circling the sky.

It's hard to imagine that the world really can change so much in one century. Will *anything* of New York's past still exist in the hundred years to come?

I pass Lexington Avenue in a trance, my eyes drinking in all of the new sights while my mind struggles to believe that what I am seeing is real. I watch as these future New Yorkers follow signs leading underground, to something called a "subway." I pass the same shop on three different blocks, each looking slightly unique yet sharing the same name: "Deli."

A delicious, buttery smell wafts toward me as I cross the street in front of a sidewalk vendor. "Get yer soft pretzels and hot dogs!" he yells. Beside him is another vendor, this one selling a vast array of magazines and newspapers. I glance at the front-page headline of the *New York Times*, which is dated February 5, 1991. *GULF WAR!* the headline screams. *Ground Troops to Enter Kuwait*, and I turn away, realizing with sadness that this new future holds no more promise of peace than my own post–Civil War era.

As I reach Fifth Avenue at Forty-Second Street, I gasp at the sight before me. The Croton Reservoir, one of my favorite places in the city, is gone. In its place is a mammoth structure covering the entire two blocks from Fortieth to Forty-Second Streets. Its façade reminds me of the Windsor Mansion, and I feel my heartbeat quicken as I wonder if I might be looking upon the Windsor home of the future. But when I look more closely, I see that the lettering on the building's exterior reads: NEW YORK PUBLIC LIBRARY. It's the biggest, grandest library I've ever seen.

Continuing up Fifth Avenue, goose bumps rise up my arms as my Christmas Eve vision is realized. The extravagant mansions and proud brownstones of the 1880s have vanished, replaced with tall buildings that house shop after shop. A massive new public plaza called Rockefeller Center decorates Midtown, and as I make my way farther up Fifth, I find that nearly every block comes equipped with its own luxury hotel, their awnings declaring such commanding names as the St. Regis and the Peninsula.

I turn onto Central Park South, and tears spring to my eyes. There it is, just ahead—the great park where some of my happiest childhood memories took place. At last, I've found a surviving friend in this unfamiliar city. And finally, *there* are the horses! I smile at the line of mares standing in front of an elegant hotel called the Plaza. If I squint hard enough, I can ignore the cars, the buildings, and all of the modern people. Keeping my eyes focused on Central Park and the horses, it looks like I could be in my own time.

A familiar marble structure, sparkling in the sunlight behind the Plaza, catches my eye. My throat suddenly turns dry. I don't want to go near it, and yet I can't stop myself. I'm running, racing across Fifty-Ninth Street, until I find myself staring at the W carved into the wrought-iron gates.

Of all the homes that have disappeared with time, the Old New York relics missing in this new world, the Windsor Mansion still stands. The white marble palace looks like a grand dame in contrast to the newer, subtler buildings that surround it.

I stand motionless at its entrance, nostalgia mixing with disgust as I gaze up at the estate. This is the place where I was betrayed, duped by the falsest of friends. It makes my skin crawl to see that there is something left of Rebecca Windsor in this new century, and as the wind ripples through the trees, I think I hear the sound of her haughty laughter.

But then Rupert's kind face fills my mind, and I feel a pang of loneliness for my friend, for all of the men and women who worked at the Windsor Mansion. They were my family. As much as the sight of the house brings back my loathing for Rebecca, it's also oddly comforting to look upon the place I once considered home. It makes me feel like less of a stranger in this new city, as though 1888 is calling out to me, saying, "I'*m still here.*"

Suddenly, my eyes lock on a figure stepping out onto Rebecca's bedroom balcony. I hold my breath, half-expecting to see my enemy. But the girl who leans over the railing, beaming as she holds a cordless telephone up to her ear, is Rebecca's complete opposite. Her auburn hair shines in the sun, and her infectious smile tugs at my insides.

She is the most beautiful girl I've ever seen. And that's when I remember my vision of the future in the Windsor Mansion secret passageway. T*his* must be the girl I was waiting for, the girl who brought me the happiness and excitement I'd never before felt.

My conscience struggles to remind me that it's useless, that I've signed contracts with the Society and promised to abide by the rules, to never stay long enough in the past or future to achieve Visibility. But it's too late. I can't turn away from what I know to be true—that I am *meant* to stay in this time and be with the girl on the balcony.

After all, I've already seen it.

## *February* 13, 1991

"Excuse me? Which way is Columbus Circle?"

I continue reading my Stephen King novel while sitting on a Central Park bench, ignoring the voice in my ear. I know the lady can't possibly be speaking to me.

"*Excuse* me?" the voice persists.

I look up slowly. Sure enough, the lady—a flustered tourist juggling a baby and two shopping bags—is staring straight at me. For a moment I can't speak.

It's finally happened. Just as the *Handbook of the Time Society* warned, I've entered Visibility after seven days in another time! Now my full form and presence have joined me in 1991, leaving 1888 behind. I know I will never be allowed into the Time Society again.

"Ah . . ." I clear my throat. After a week of being silent, it's a shock to hear my own voice. "You'll want to leave the park through Artist's Gate, there on the right. Stay on Central Park South until you reach Eighth Avenue, and there you'll see Columbus Circle." As she thanks me and hurries off, I marvel at the incredible fact that I've just given directions to a place that doesn't even *exist* in my own time!

I've spent the past week immersed in the 1990s, my invisibility allowing me to experience the modern world uninhibited. I slipped into Broadway theaters and movie Cineplexes, watching in openmouthed awe as a helicopter landed on the stage right in front of me during the live musical *Miss Saigon*, and hardly breathing while experiencing my first motion picture, *Edward Scissorhands*. I rode the subway, holding on to the railing for dear life as the car sped through darkness, and visited the two museums that survived all the way from my time: the American Museum of Natural History and the Metropolitan Museum of Art. The sight of these stalwart institutions filled me with joy, and I spent two long days examining their collections, learning all that I could about life in the future.

On my first evening in 1991, I came up with a rather ingenious idea of where to stay the night. I wandered into the hotel next to Windsor Mansion, the Plaza, and by listening in on the conversation at the reception desk, learned which rooms were vacant. My evenings at the hotel were like something out of a dream. The room that I invisibly occupied had an icebox filled to the brim with chocolates, snacks, and beverages, a real stand-up shower and no shortage of hot water, the most plush bed I've ever slept in, and television—which I'm beginning to find quite entertaining.

But now, my invisibility has run out and it's time to find more conventional means of lodging. Since my arrival, I've quickly discovered that hotel rooms in Manhattan are far beyond my budget. Though I borrowed 1990s dollars from the Aura currency exchange, the entire amount would be lost in just one week if I stayed at a hotel in the city.

It's time to take my 1990s experience to the next level: by finding a roommate.

## February 14, 1991

I arrive early for my very first photography class at the Museum of Modern Art, passing unusual and eye-catching exhibition halls before reaching the Study Center. The vast space is decorated with an assortment of framed black-and-white and color photographs lining the walls, while a dozen empty desks fill the room. I glance up at the colorful day calendar adorning the teacher's desk, opened to the date February 14, and realize with a jolt of surprise that today is Valentine's Day.

The holiday completely slipped my mind. I'd never been able to get away from it in my old Time, from the annual homemade card exchange in the servants' quarters of the Windsor house, to the Valentine's dances at boarding school and Cornell. I always thought it a rather silly holiday, but it gladdens me to know that it is still celebrated an entire century later. These days, I find myself savoring any link between my time and the new.

I find a seat at one of the desks, pulling my brand-new Kodak camera out of my backpack. As I adjust the lens I watch a group of students of various ages filter into the room, chatting and exchanging Valentine's Day greetings before settling into their seats. I feel curious eyes on me, and I smile at the group self-consciously before fixing my eyes back on the gadget in my hands.

Someone new walks in and I freeze, my face still pressed against the camera. I stare at her through the lens, feeling my breath escape me.

Auburn hair flows over her shoulders in waves, framing porcelain skin, while the sparkle in her hazel eyes makes me long to know what she is thinking. Her infectious smile gives me the same tug in my chest that I felt when looking upon the girl on the balcony of Windsor Mansion, on my first day in 1991.

*It is the same girl.*

I lower my camera, unable to take my eyes off of her. She walks by my chair, giving me a curious grin, and my cheeks grow warm as her radiance is directed at me.

"Hi. I'm Marion Windsor."

*Marion Windsor.* She belongs to that family and yet she seems so different from them, so warm and enchanting.

I quickly take off my cap, standing to greet her. "I'm Henry Irving."

Her smile widens and she looks at me as if she knows something I don't. It takes all of my self-control not to reach over to touch the dimple in her cheek, to take her porcelain hand in mine. It's then that I realize—she is the reason I was meant to time travel. And now that I've found her, I can't imagine ever going back.

## May 31, 1993

"*Don't go changing to try and please me . . .*," I croon to Marion with a grin, twirling her around on the sidewalk after the Billy Joel concert. She giggles, tucking her head into my shoulder.

"That show was beyond amazing," she says dreamily. "'And So It Goes' is definitely one of my new favorite songs."

We take turns goofily serenading each other with selections from Billy Joel's set list as we make the long walk from Madison

Square Garden back to Windsor Mansion. The warm late-spring night feels full of promise, and I find myself glancing down at Marion's hand every so often, smiling at the plastic ring on her finger. We picked it out together after I proposed, cracking up as we chose among the fake diamonds for sale on Canal Street. It was Marion's idea—I wanted to give her the best ring I could afford, but she insisted on saving the money for our life together. The plastic bauble on her finger is a constant reminder of the happiest day of my life, of our secret engagement, and of the future with her that I can't wait to begin.

As we turn onto Fifth Avenue, I hear an unmistakable voice behind me.

"Funny seeing you here."

The sound turns my blood cold. My body stiffens, seizing with panic. It's a voice I haven't heard since my former life in 1888, belonging to someone who should be long dead by now.

*It can't be her*, I tell myself as I slowly turn around.

A strangled cry escapes me as I stare into the chilling, dark pools of her eyes. It's her—Rebecca Windsor, her face ghastlier than I remembered, her tall figure menacing as it moves toward us. How could she be in the future, looking as young as the day I last saw her?

*She's a ghost*, I realize with horror.

"Henry? Henry!" I snap back to attention at the sound of Marion calling my name and tugging my sleeve, her face furrowed with worry. "What's wrong?"

"I—I thought someone was trying to mug us," I improvise lamely, forcing a chuckle.

Marion rolls her eyes at me fondly. I wrap my arm around

her protectively, glancing back one more time and shuddering at the sight of Rebecca's ghost trailing us and smirking at my fear. I keep my eyes focused straight ahead, struggling to stay present in my conversation with Marion as my mind whirs. *Why is she here? What does she want? How can I keep Marion safe now that Rebecca's seen her?*

At last we reach Windsor Mansion, Rebecca's ominous presence still darkening the sidewalk behind us. For the first time, as I say good night to Marion I'm glad of her parents' strict rule forbidding me from being with her past eleven p.m. I need to see her safely inside, away from Rebecca's ghost.

Once the front doors close behind Marion, I turn to face Rebecca, my muscles trembling with fury and fear.

"What are you doing here?" I growl at her.

"That's no way to greet the fiancée you haven't seen in a century." Rebecca's eyes flash with anger as she looks up at Windsor Mansion. "I see you've missed me—that can be your only explanation for going after my descendant. A pathetic replacement for the original."

"Go haunt someone else, Rebecca," I shoot back. "I've wanted nothing to do with you since the day we last saw each other."

"Haunt someone else?" Rebecca echoes, a grotesque smile spreading across her face. "Why, I'm no ghost, Irving. I'm like you. A time traveler." She turns her head to the side, and I watch in horror as a brief flash of a gold key swings from beneath her blouse.

"What did you do?" I demand, panic coursing through me. "Whose key did you steal?"

Rebecca laughs lightly. "All that matters is what *you* are going to do now, old friend. You see, I won't accept my future family being marred by the likes of you." Her eyes narrow into slits and she takes a step closer. "If you want your little girl-friend to see her next birthday, then you'll leave, Irving. You'll go back to where you came from—and never return, never see her again."

My throat is painfully dry as I stare at her.

"Fine. I'll leave. But you have to give me a little time."

"The longer you take, the bigger the risk." Rebecca flashes her teeth in an ominous smile. "I'll see you back in 'eighty-eight. Alone."

I watch in despair as her image flickers and vanishes into the night. I can't leave Marion, I could never hurt her like that. I don't think I'd ever survive it myself. But I can't stay here either, not with Rebecca at large and Marion approaching her line of fire.

I only hope Los Angeles is far enough away that I can out-smart Rebecca and keep Marion safe.

A Timekeeper can exist beyond her death only if her younger self travels forward in time, past the end of her life. Even then, death has still occurred. The deceased Timekeeper can no longer live in the Natural Timeline.

—THE HANDBOOK OF THE TIME SOCIETY

# 14

## Present Day

Philip strode into the Osborne after school, smiling as he remembered the way Michele had looked at him that day during lunch, how right it had felt to be so close to her. It was hard to believe he'd initially been able to keep her at bay—he was already counting the hours until he'd get to see her again in the morning.

Philip had never imagined himself to be one of those New Age-y guys who believed in the paranormal . . . but he couldn't seem to deny what was happening. He found himself remembering bits and pieces of his history with Michele the more time he spent with her, and with every new fragment of memory, his feelings strengthened.

Clambering up the stairs to the second-floor apartment, Philip's mind was already ahead of him at the piano. He could feel a composition coming on, and his fingers buzzed in anticipation. Tossing his backpack on the floor, Philip dashed to the piano. But just before his hands hit the keys, he heard a sound—a scratching, clawing noise coming from the adjacent living room. Philip moved toward it, grimacing as he wondered if he was about to be met by an infestation of rats. But what he saw instead caused him to stop dead in his tracks.

The wall was moving and shuddering, letters carving into its surface by an unseen hand. The letters *B* and *R* jutted out of the wall, and Philip watched, transfixed, as an invisible phantom carved the words *BROOKLYN BRIDGE 11 P.M.*—*in his own handwriting.*

Michele returned home, lost in thought about all she'd learned at the Time Society. She felt older somehow, as if the day's discoveries had aged her. The idea that half of her belonged in this present day and the other half in 1904 was chilling and made her feel like some kind of freak experiment. How was she going to explain *this* one to Philip? At a certain point, wasn't he going to want a normal relationship—with someone who had just one Timeline and didn't bring a bunch of supernatural elements to the table?

"You're home!" she heard Dorothy call out with relief from the open door of the drawing room.

"Hi," Michele responded, joining her grandparents.

"Any luck with Elizabeth?" Walter asked. She could tell he was still skeptical.

"Yeah, actually. We discovered that I have a special time-travel power . . . one that could be really helpful," Michele shared. "And I think it's time I take one last journey before Rebecca reaches her full power tomorrow."

"Where's that?" Walter asked worriedly.

"I have to see my dad."

Before climbing into the passageway to make the switch to her alternate Time, Michele's cell phone beeped with a text. A smile lit up her face as she saw Philip's name on the screen. She clicked to open the message.

*She's going to be at the Brooklyn Bridge tomorrow at 11 p.m.,* it read. *We need to meet her there. That's when we're supposed to finish this.*

Michele's eyes widened as she read the words.

*How do you know?* she typed back.

*Philip—the old me—sent me a message. If you can believe that.*

Michele's breath caught in her throat. *I believe it.*

Slipping her phone into her pocket, her hands shaking with anticipation, she pushed the glass-enclosed bookcase until it swung to the side. As she jumped into the passageway, she whispered like an incantation, "Take me to my father—to my other Timeline."

*"East side, west side, all around the town*
*The tots sang 'ring-around-rosie,' 'London Bridge is*
*falling down. . . .'"*

Michele's head snapped up at the sound of a child's singing coming from the library. For a moment she faltered, wondering if she'd once again inadvertently returned to her father and Rebecca's childhood. But then she peeked through a crack in the bookcase and saw four-year-old Frances "Frankie" Windsor singing to her doll, while an eleven-year-old Violet Windsor and a sour-faced tutor hunkered over a French book.

"Quiet, Frances!" Michele heard the tutor admonish, then return to Violet. *"Répétez, s'il vous plaît: Je m'appelle Violet."*

Michele hurried to the end of the tunnel, hoisting herself above the ground and onto the grass. She made her way through the back lawn toward the front of the house, breathing in the fresh turn-of-the-century air. *Please let my dad be here,* she silently prayed as she slipped through the front doors and into the Grand Hall. *Please.*

A young maid descended the staircase holding a tray filled with discarded plates and silverware, while a footman pushed a tea cart toward the drawing room. Invisible to them both, Michele followed the footman, brimming with hopeful anticipation. But the drawing room was occupied by only the lady of the house, Henrietta Windsor, and a female guest. Michele crept out of the room, suddenly thinking of the servants' quarters. *He might be visiting Rupert!*

Michele realized with consternation that she had never been to the servants' area and had no clue how to get there. She tore through the first floor, her heart hammering in her chest as she searched for stairs leading below. In the dining room, she finally found what she was looking for: a gilded door at the back of the room that blended in with the rest of the walls but swung open to reveal a butler's pantry. It was the size of a modest kitchen and was filled with floor-to-ceiling glass cabinets that held all the Windsor china and dinnerware. A second swinging door in the butler's pantry led to the belowstairs section of the house.

*He has to be there,* Michele thought eagerly, taking the steps two at a time. She wound up in a large, dim room with a long table and chairs in the center. It looked like a staff dining or recreation room—but it was empty. She heard a cacophony of voices coming from the next room, and she quickly rounded the corner, finding herself in a vast kitchen, where a matronly cook was barking orders at a team of kitchen and scullery maids. Still Irving Henry was nowhere in sight.

Suddenly, the cook and maids stood to attention, looking through Michele at someone just behind her. She whirled around to see who it was, and her heart sank. The man behind her was clearly the butler—his black-tie uniform and the staff's deferential demeanor toward him made that evident—but he wasn't old enough to be Rupert, the butler Irving had known.

The cook gave him a respectful nod. "Do we have the final tally for dinner yet, Martin?"

"Yes, we do. The table will be set for six tonight," Martin announced. "Mr. Henry is staying to dinner."

Michele's heart nearly stopped

"It's a good thing I'm making his favorite stew," the cook

said fondly. "I didn't know Mr. Henry was back or I'd have prepared a plate of fresh shortbread for his tea."

"He only just arrived, and the footman is serving him tea on the lawn now," Martin told her. "But I'm sure the short-bread would be welcome tomorrow if he stays the night—"

Michele didn't wait a second longer. She bolted through the servants' hall and up the stairs, past the butler's pantry and into the dining room; then she dashed through the Grand Hall and outside to the back lawn, feeling her heart almost burst out of her chest when she saw the man in the distance, sitting in a wicker chair, his eyes closed as he tilted his face to the sky.

She drew closer, holding her breath. Irving Henry opened his eyes at the sound of her approach. He stared at Michele and she gazed back at him, soaking in every detail of finally looking upon her father—in person. Irving Henry had aged, but he was still handsome. In his face, Michele could see a lingering shadow of the boy her mother had loved.

When he broke the silence, his voice was incredulous, hopeful, and familiar.

*"Marion?"*

Michele struggled to speak. "N-no. I'm not Marion."

Irving peered closer at her. His eyes filled with disbelief as he saw his face reflected in hers.

"The Vanishing Girl," he murmured. "The Vanishing Girl from the park." He sat up straighter.

"You *remember*," Michele breathed, looking at him in amazement. "I can't believe you remember that day."

Irving's face tensed and Michele could almost see him remembering his companion from that day; she could practically feel him wondering if she was there because of Rebecca.

"Who are you really?"

And Michele said the words she had imagined saying all her life.

"My name is Michele Windsor. I'm your daughter.'"

Irving gasped. He stared at her in astonishment, uncertainty momentarily flickering in his eyes—but then, as he looked into her face that so resembled his own, conviction took hold.

"I . . . I have a daughter?" His voice was barely above a whisper.

Michele shakily lifted her necklace, showing him the key. Irving dropped to his knees at the sight, tears glistening in his eyes.

"I don't understand. How could I have never known about you?" he asked, looking at her as if afraid she might disappear.

"My mom didn't know she was pregnant until—until you left."

"My daughter—you're my daughter," he echoed dazedly.

Irving let out a sob. Slowly he stood, and then he had his arms around her, hugging her as tears spilled from her eyes onto his sleeve.

"Dad," Michele cried, "I finally found you!"

Irving's body shook as he spoke. "Leaving Marion was the worst mistake I ever made. I thought it would only be temporary, that I was protecting her. I thought the key would lead her back to me. But I was wrong, and my biggest regret is the time I lost with her—and now, with you." He looked at her intently.

"Where is she? *How* is she? I've waited so long—I would give anything to see her again."

Michele couldn't speak. As she looked away, Irving shook his head frantically, fighting off comprehending such a terrible truth.

"No—no, it can't be," he whispered. "Not Marion."

"It was a car accident." Michele's throat was thick with tears. "Two months ago. That's why I had to move here. That's why I have your key. It was in her safe—she never realized what it was."

Irving looked at her desperately, his eyes seeming to beg her to tell him it wasn't true, that Marion was still alive.

"I never stopped loving her," he said after a long pause. "From the moment I returned to my Time, I knew I might not see her again. But all the years that passed didn't change a thing. I've thought of Marion every minute, I've missed her every day. I became a lawyer for the Windsor family just so that I could feel closer to her. I only left to protect her, to give her a better future. I suppose it never occurred to me . . . that I would fail."

"You were protecting her from Rebecca, weren't you?" Michele asked.

Irving looked at her sharply, his forehead creasing with worry. "What do you know about Rebecca?"

"I read the journals that you left for my mom. But it's more than that." Michele took a deep breath. "Rebecca is out there in the future, in my Time, and she wants me dead. The new president of the Time Society told me that Rebecca murdered

Millicent August in 1910 and stole her key. That's how she's been able to time travel and Age Shift into my time."

Irving's face paled. He seized Michele's hand. "Stay here in 1904 with me," he pleaded. "I can shield you from her; she won't even know you yet. Please, don't go back if she's after you. Let me protect you, the way I meant to protect Marion."

"I can't stay," Michele told him regretfully. "She's threatening my grandparents and my friends; I can't leave them while she's out there. And tomorrow, we might have a chance to finally end this. We're meeting her on the Brooklyn Bridge. I'll have help with me—don't worry."

"I can't stand knowing you're in danger. It's all my fault." Irving looked at her desperately. "Please—there has to be something I can do."

Michele remembered Ida's words, but she hesitated to repeat them. She had only just met her father; she couldn't bear to have him risk his life for her.

"I have nothing left," Irving said quietly. "I lost Marion, and now that I've found you—I couldn't bear losing you too. If there's even the slightest chance of my being able to help, I *must* do so."

Michele blinked back a fresh wave of tears.

"The new president of the Time Society, Ida Pearl, told me that Millicent had this theory. . . . She believed that an Age Shifting Timekeeper would have to—to die in multiple Timelines besides their own in order to be gone for good." She shivered. "I have no idea how it would work, and I can't even imagine being responsible for someone's death."

Irving's face filled with determination.

"You could never be responsible. This is all Rebecca's doing. We *have* to do whatever we can to end this, to protect you. I knew Millicent, and I would trust in any theory she had." He thought quickly. "I could trick Rebecca into meeting me on the Brooklyn Bridge the same day as you—only in our time. If I can defeat her in my time and you succeed in yours, then if Millicent's theory is correct . . . this could be the end of Rebecca."

"I got a . . . a tip that she would be there on November 23, in my time, at eleven p.m." Michele looked up at her father, overwhelmed with emotion. "I wish you didn't have to see Rebecca again. I'm afraid of what that will be like for you."

"There's no need to worry. I'm glad to do anything I can to protect you." As Irving looked at her, it seemed to Michele that he could see into her thoughts. "Is there something else bothering you?" he asked gently.

Michele nodded slowly.

"When I found your journals in the passageway this week, I was so grateful I got to hear your story and learn about you. I only wish Mom had been the one to find them." She lowered her eyes. "I went to the Time Society after learning about them from your writings, and the president told me that as a time-crossed child, I'll be involuntarily split between your Time and my mom's, traveling against my will. It's already started." She looked up at her father fearfully. "I don't know how to control it."

"Oh, Michele." Irving's voice broke. "I'm so sorry—I didn't know. I never meant for you to have this burden. But now that I've met you . . . you're perfect, and I know that you were meant to be here, to do great things with your gifts and your life. I promise—I will do everything I can to try and help you."

Michele smiled, moved by his words.

"There is one bit of hope. Today I learned I can travel without a key just like your father could."

She watched as Irving's eyes grew wide and he beamed with pride.

"Unbelievable! You can't imagine how many times I've tried to do the same since leaving the 1990s, yet I've never been able to time travel without the key. The gift must have skipped a generation. You're my father's granddaughter indeed." He gazed at her fondly.

"But if you can't travel without the key, how did you return to 1888 after leaving it behind for my mom?" Michele asked.

"I held on to the key while beginning my Time jump, dropping it only after I felt myself moving into the air. The physics professor I worked for at the time was my one confidant—he believed in time travel and was fascinated by my story. He took the key as it fell from my hand, and he was to make sure Marion received it. I wonder, when he saw that I didn't return and Marion never left . . . why didn't he tell her the truth?"

"I looked him up when I found the note he left for my mom along with the key. He died after a years-long battle from a stroke," Michele explained sadly. "He must have never had the chance to talk to her."

Irving clasped both her hands in his. "Your mother and I . . . our story is a tragedy, and I feel the pain and loss every single day. But you—you are the ray of light in all this.

Discovering you now . . . it makes everything seem all right. Millicent always said the most skilled Timekeepers were the ones who could travel even without their key—like a wizard able to do magic without a wand. Time-crossed or not, you are powerful," he told her firmly. "I know you will be able to have the full life you want and deserve, regardless of what the Time Society says."

"Thank you . . . Dad. You don't know how much I needed to hear that. And now that we know I can travel without the key . . ." Michele reached around her neck to unfasten the necklace, but Irving stopped her.

"No, it's yours. I want to know that you'll always have it with you, if ever something should happen and you need it. Besides, you're meant to hand it down to your own child one day."

His image began to waver in front of her, his voice faint as he said something she couldn't hear, and Michele reached out for him, desperate to keep her father with her for just a little longer.

"Dad, I can feel it—I'm going back!" she cried out.

He pulled her into one last hug. "I'm sorry I didn't know you until now," he said intently. "But this isn't the end. You can always find me. The past is open to you. You are a Timekeeper. And I will do everything I can from here, to help you succeed. My daughter, I love you."

Michele smiled through her tears. "I love you too."

And then she felt her body begin to hover above the ground, her father's image blurring, until he was gone and she knew with certainty that she was back in her own Time.

# DAY SEVEN

Michele awoke feeling like the world had somehow changed overnight. The sky was a darker, duller gray with not a trace of sun, and the usually speeding cars and squealing sirens of Manhattan were uncharacteristically quiet. It was as though the city were hiding in anticipation of Rebecca's impending Visibility.

This time Michele relented when Walter and Dorothy asked her to stay home from school. She hated to think about it, but should Rebecca succeed that night, Michele wanted her grandparents to have one last memory with her. The three of them spent the day huddled together, talking about everything: their memories of Marion, Michele's meeting with Irving, and her relationship with Philip. It would have been her most special day ever spent with Walter and Dorothy, if it weren't for the event that lay ahead.

Philip pulled up in his Audi at dinnertime, and as Michele introduced him to her grandparents, she thought how surreal and strange it was that their first meeting should be taking place before this impending fight against Rebecca. Walter and Dorothy had listened in astonishment to Michele's story over dinner the previous night, when she revealed her relationship with Philip and his knowledge of Rebecca. She could tell they'd been frightened by the idea of history repeating itself with another romance across time, but they also seemed to find comfort in Philip's potential to help her.

After a tense dinner where none of them managed to eat, the four of them piled into Philip's car, Michele taking the front seat. As they were driving, Philip placed a reassuring hand over hers, and she marveled at her ability to feel sparks from his touch, even at a moment like this.

## 1953

Philip Walker buttoned up his overcoat and wrapped his scarf more tightly around his neck, trying to fend off the sudden, fierce gusts of wind. He'd certainly picked the wrong day to go for a brisk walk over the Brooklyn Bridge. Only a few pedestrians joined him and he could hear their disgruntled mutterings about the weather.

*I'm already halfway across. No sense in backing out now,* Philip thought with a shrug, and he continued along the path.

## 1904

Irving waited in tense anticipation at the walkway in the center of the Brooklyn Bridge. Would Rebecca come? He'd sent a telegram to meet on the bridge and never heard back, though he knew she always liked to keep people on their toes. After all these years, he imagined she'd be too curious to refuse. He tapped his foot nervously while he waited, his thoughts more than a hundred years in the future with his daughter.

## 2010

After parking the car, Philip, Walter, and Dorothy surrounded Michele, rallying around her as they stepped onto the bridge. The four of them moved toward the railing, and Philip's fingers laced with hers as they looked out over the darkened East River. For one brief moment Michele let down her guard, pretending they were on a date rather than on this dreaded outing. And then she heard her grandmother scream.

## 1904

Irving's spine stiffened as the hateful vision came into focus: a tall, stately figure with a mass of black hair and feral dark eyes, stalking toward him. He fought a wave of nausea, his hands balling into fists, as she came closer.

"Irving Henry. I knew you missed me."

The intimacy in her voice was repugnant. Irving forced himself to stay calm, to meet her eyes. As he looked into them, he drew back in horror at what he saw.

## 1953

Philip Walker felt eyes boring into him. He turned to see one of the other pedestrians glaring at him with distaste. He peered closer, doing a double take in alarm. Was it really . . . ? *Yes.* It was Rebecca Windsor, the very person Michele had warned him about twenty years ago. Philip hadn't seen Rebecca in nearly a half-century, yet still Rebecca recognized him, eyeing him with hatred. Philip's heartbeat quickened with fear as he remembered Michele's words. *"She wants me dead."*

## 2010

Michele and Philip spun around at the sound of Dorothy's screams, then clung to each other as the figure from their nightmares advanced toward them. Rebecca looked frighteningly powerful in her full human form, her body tall and sturdy with black curls coiling around her hostile face like snakes, her eyes black pools. She wielded a fire torch in her hands, and Michele cried out at the sight of her grandmother—hunched over in agony as Rebecca's flames burned at her feet. Michele raced to her side, just as Rebecca dropped a second torch, directly hitting Michele's leg. Michele screamed in pain, her legs buckling beneath her as the fire burned. She heard Philip yelling as she hit the ground; she could hear him and Walter struggling to stamp on the flames surrounding her and Dorothy. In the split second Michele and her protectors had their eyes down, fighting the fire, Rebecca moved in behind her. And the sharp blade of a knife sliced into Michele's side.

Michele howled in pain. This was it, she was going to die. She watched in horror as blood seeped through her shirt, the fire still enveloping her jeans.

Over Dorothy's screams and Philip's roar of rage, she heard a cold voice say the words, "At last." The final thing Michele saw before blacking out was Rebecca Windsor brandishing the bloodied knife, her savage eyes gleaming.

## 1904

Irving trembled with fury as he looked at Rebecca, the vision filling his mind: Michele, doubled over on the Brooklyn Bridge, covered in blood and flames while Rebecca stood over her with the blade. He had to do something—he *had* to stop it.

"Well? Aren't you going to say anything?" Rebecca smirked. "You haven't seen me in sixteen years."

Irving seized her with a force he never knew he had, pushing her up against the railing of the bridge.

"You will *never*. Hurt. My. Daughter," he growled in her ear, before throwing her over.

## 2010

*"NO!"* Philip cried in agony. Watching Michele passed out and bleeding on the burning bridge, he felt as if he were being split in two. The sight of Rebecca's smile set him over the edge. He let out a strangled yell and lunged toward her, catching her off guard. Gathering every ounce of his strength, Philip lifted her body. Walter rushed forward to help shoulder the weight, and the two of them hoisted her into the air—pushing her over the Brooklyn Bridge before she had the chance to harm Michele again.

## 1953

It happened so fast. Philip's mouth fell open in shock as he watched what looked like an invisible hand *pushing* Rebecca over the bridge. One moment she was there, walking toward him—the next she was dead in the waters below. He backed away from the sight.

*Did I do that?* It wasn't possible. But then . . . who? How?

Philip hurried forward, anxious to get far away from Rebecca's final standing place. As he ran to the end of the bridge, a thought floated through his mind, flooding him with relief.

*Michele is going to be okay; she's safe. Rebecca can never hurt her again.*

## 2010

As Rebecca's body hit the East River, Millicent's key at long last snapped off the thief's neck, flying straight up into the sky.

Michele's eyelids fluttered. As Walter frantically dialed 911, Philip joined Dorothy, who was leaning over her, holding her wounded body.

"It's over now," Philip told her, reaching for her hand. "She'll never hurt you—or your family—ever again."

The Natural Timeline is another word for Fate. This is life without the interference of time travelers; where Timekeepers may observe events out of sequence on the Natural Timeline, but they do not affect it.

If a Timekeeper does somehow effect change, have they altered Fate? Or did Fate intend on the Timekeeper's actions all along?

This question is still up for debate—though I have to admit, my belief leans toward the latter.

—THE HANDBOOK OF THE TIME SOCIETY

A soft knock sounded at the door of Michele's room at Lenox
Hill Hospital.

"Come in," she called, glancing beside her and smiling to
see Philip still asleep on the visitor's chair.

As her guest walked into the room, bearing a huge bouquet
of flowers, Michele sat up straighter, her eyes wide.

"Ida Pearl!"

"Hello, dear," Ida said warmly, standing over the hospital
bed. "How are you feeling?"

"Better every day." Michele smiled bravely.

"I came as soon as I heard." She paused. "I believe I owe
you a thank-you . . . and an apology. Because of you, Millicent's key is no longer giving power to a madwoman. You've

restored a sense of order to our world—you and your young man." Ida smiled at the sleeping Philip.

"My dad too," Michele added. "I know he helped from 1904, just like he promised."

"We were wrong about you and Irving," Ida confessed. "I see that now, and I hope you can accept my apology, and invitation to join the Time Society."

"I'd be glad to join—especially if you can help me." Michele's expression grew serious. "As much as I love experiencing history and traveling back in time, I want to live in the present with Philip. I don't want to have to worry about time-crossing to 1904, I just want to live in the here and now. Do you think you can help?"

"I promise to try," Ida agreed. "The fact that you can travel without a key shows that you have a higher level of power than most Timekeepers. We might want to schedule some private lessons for honing your skills. I wouldn't be surprised with the talent you've already shown, if you can find a way to control this."

Michele let out a sigh of relief. "Thank you. And . . . there's something else."

"Yes?"

"If like you said, breaking the Society laws isn't always bad . . . then what would happen if I went back and tried to stop my mom's accident?" Michele looked up hopefully at the Time Society president. She had wondered about this often since discovering she could time travel. Though she'd dreamt of her mother telling her not to tamper with destiny, that it had been her time to go, Michele still wasn't able to accept it.

Ida sighed. "I'm afraid that wouldn't be possible. It creates a paradox."

"What do you mean?"

"Your mother's death is what caused you to discover the key and your power. Therefore, you can't go back and stop the very event that enables you to travel in the first place," Ida explained. "You can try, but when it comes to paradoxes like these, no matter what you do the outcome is always the same." She reached over to give Michele's shoulder a comforting squeeze. "The only thing you *can* do is aim for acceptance."

"That hasn't been easy," she said quietly. "My mom was my best friend."

"I understand. But you know better than anyone that Time and Death are ultimately illusions. Those we've loved and lost can never truly be gone when the past still exists. It's just another layer of the universe."

Michele was silent, contemplating Ida's words, when a question occurred to her.

"Do you have any idea what happened to Millicent's key? Philip and my grandparents all saw it sail into the air as Rebecca fell . . . but they didn't see where it went."

"We don't know either," Ida admitted. "We're assigning nearly all of our Timekeepers on missions to different places to try to locate it. But the most important thing is that it's no longer with Rebecca."

"You can say that again," Michele agreed.

"I'll see you soon, I hope. Are your wounds patching up all right? If not we have a couple of incredible doctors in the Society—"

"I'm fine," she giggled. "As much as I'd *love* a time traveler operating on me, my abdomen is thankfully starting to heal, and my jeans caught the brunt of the fire—I don't have any permanent burns."

"Glad to hear it. And congratulations, Michele. You've proven yourself a very special and capable Timekeeper." With one last smile of approval, Ida was out the door, followed shortly by a red-eyed Caissie Hart.

"Hey," Michele greeted her, taken aback.

Caissie burst into tears.

"It's okay, I'm alive."

"No, I'm *so sorry,*" Caissie cried. "It makes me sick to think I *helped* that psychopath. If I'd only known . . . but either way, I was wrong. I just wish we could go back to being friends."

"Maybe we can. I don't know," Michele said honestly. "But I believe you that you didn't mean for anything like this to happen."

"I'm going to make it up to you," Caissie vowed. "Somehow I will."

Philip finally stirred. "Oh, hey, Caissie," he murmured through a yawn, before turning on his side and falling back to sleep.

Michele and Caissie glanced at each other and laughed.

"He's keeping quite a vigil," Caissie said with a grin.

"He's been amazing," Michele agreed, "especially considering he saved my life. And the most unbelievable part of all is that it *was* him all along . . . the same Philip, in a new lifetime."

One week later Michele was home from the hospital, and with the exception of a giant bandage still covering her abdomen, was nearly back to normal. She lay on the couch in her sitting room with her head nestled in Dorothy's lap while they watched a soapy BBC miniseries. Walter sat in the armchair beside them, next to the silver-framed photo of Irving Henry that he and Dorothy had gifted to Michele while she was in the hospital. As the end credits rolled on the TV screen, Michele heard a familiar knock at the door.

"Come on in," she called, her spirits instantly lifting. Philip walked into the room, and Michele's face lit up. Despite the wreckage Rebecca caused for her family, and the hurdles she knew that still lay ahead, Michele felt like one of the luckiest girls in the world. The boy she loved, the boy she had followed across time, had come back to her and was ready to face this new future together.

"I think we have some business to tend to with Annaleigh," said her grandmother, rising. "Right, Walter?"

"Um, right. We'll see you two later, then."

Michele and Philip chuckled as Walter and Dorothy strode out of the room.

"They think they're being so smooth," Michele said fondly, stepping closer to Philip. "So, what's up?"

"I have something to give you," said Philip, and with a smile he slipped the signet ring off his finger. "I think this belongs to you."

Michele looked up at him, her eyes shining. "I don't know what to say."

"Then don't say anything," he murmured, his face leaning closer to hers.

Michele closed her eyes, her body tensing in anticipation as slowly, gently, he brushed his lips against hers. She felt herself gasp and suddenly they were kissing, his lips caressing her neck and collarbone while she ran her fingers through his hair. He pulled her closer, and as their lips met again and again, she longed to capture this moment forever.

When they finally managed to break away, Philip clasped her hand. "Are you ready?"

She knew what he meant. Was she prepared to assume the life of a Timekeeper, while also juggling the roles of Windsor heiress and high-school student? Was she ready to face her destiny—past, present, and future?

She looked up at him, her eyes bright.

"Of course . . . I'm with you."

# AUTHOR'S NOTE

While I was writing *Timeless*, my historical research was all consuming—I felt like I was traveling back in time with Michele! When I began this sequel, I revisited my previous research and explored some new areas. Below are my resources.

## OLD NEW YORK AND GILDED AGE LIFE

As in *Timeless*, the ever-changing New York setting is a constant theme in *Timekeeper*. I rented an apartment in Manhattan while writing *Timeless*, and the greatest research truly was just living and breathing the city, exploring all the neighborhoods and landmarks, and learning New York inside out. Especially helpful in my research were the New York Historical Society, the Museum of the City of New York, and the New York Public Library.

Much of *Timekeeper* takes place early in the Gilded Age, in 1888—more than twenty years before Michele's time travel destinations in *Timeless*. To immerse myself in Gilded Age New York, I reread several books written about or set in this era. Some of my recommendations: *A Season of Splendor: The Gilded Age in the Court of Mrs. Astor* by Greg King; *Consuelo and Alva Vanderbilt: The Story of a Daughter and a Mother in the Gilded Age* by Amanda Mackenzie Stuart; *Fortune's Children: The Fall of the House of Vanderbilt* by Arthur T. Vanderbilt II, *When the Astors Owned New York: Blue Bloods and Grand Hotels in a Gilded Age* by Justin Kaplan; *The Custom of the Country* by Edith Wharton; and *Prelude to the Century: 1870–1900*, part of Time-Life's *Our American Century* series. I also studied the excellent documentary *New York*, directed by Ken Burns.

## THE WINDSOR MANSION

The Fifth Avenue mansions of old New York are unfortunately no longer standing, but you can catch a thrilling glimpse of what those homes were like by visiting Newport, Rhode Island. The Preservation Society of Newport County saved and fully preserved some of the most jaw-dropping summerhouses owned by New York families such as the Vanderbilts and the Astors. I took a research trip to Newport while writing *Timeless*, and I based the Windsor Mansion on two different Vanderbilt homes there: Alva Vanderbilt's Marble House and Alice Vanderbilt's The Breakers. Both Marble House and The Breakers were designed and built by America's king of Gilded Age architecture, Richard Morris Hunt, while Jules Allard and Sons were in charge of interior decoration. The Windsor Mansion's Grand Hall was inspired by a similar entrance vestibule at The Breakers, while I based the mansion's exterior on that of Marble House. I highly recommend a visit to Newport, but you can also visit the sights from afar by checking out the Preservation Society's books and DVD on the mansions—and check out *newportmansions.org*!

A&E's *America's Castles* DVD series also has a great episode on the Newport Mansions and their illustrious owners.

## THE OSBORNE

A good deal of action in this story takes place at the Osborne, a designated landmark apartment building in New York City. My mentor, composer Maury Yeston, lives in the Osborne, and every time I visited, I was always in awe of the building's grandeur and history. I'm grateful to Maury for inspiring me to incorporate the Osborne into the story, and for introducing me to the building's historian, Lester Barnett. I'm so appreciative of Lester's sharing his extensive knowledge of the Osborne's history with me, and showing me his preserved Victorian-era apartment! Further information and photos of the Osborne are available online.

## ORIGINAL MUSIC

In *Timeless*, Michele and Philip fall in love while writing music together. They collaborate on two songs in the book, "Bring The Colors Back" and "Chasing Time." Being a singer/songwriter myself, I was inspired to write and record their songs, to give readers the full experience! I wrote the lyrics first, and then composed the music with songwriters Heather Holley and Michael Bearden. Michael then produced the tracks. I was so fortunate to be able to record these songs with the most incredible ten-piece orchestra!

In *Timekeeper*, Michele and twenty-first-century Philip write a new song together, called "I Remember." I wrote and recorded this song as well. You can check out all songs from the Timeless series on iTunes and at my website, alexandramonir.com. I hope you enjoy them!

For more reflections and updates on the series, stay in touch with me on my website, on Facebook (facebook.com/Timeless-Series), and on Twitter at @TimelessAlex. Thank you so much, and happy reading!

# ACKNOWLEDGMENTS

It's been an incredibly special two years since *Timeless* was first published, and I have so many people to thank! My love and appreciation first and foremost go to all the *Timeless* fans. Thank you for embracing this story, and for your sweet messages that have brought me so many smiles! I wrote this book with all of you in my mind and heart.

To the best publishing team an author could ever wish for, Beverly Horowitz and Krista Vitola: You've made big dreams of mine come true, and I am so grateful for you both. Beverly, thank you for taking me under your wing. Your guidance and belief in me means the world! Krista, thank you for being a brilliant, wonderful editor. Working with you is such a joy!

I couldn't have asked for a more romantic cover, and for that I have to thank Vikki Sheatsley for the gorgeous design and Chad Michael Ward for the beautiful photography. Amanda Hong and Colleen Fellingham, I'm in awe of your copyediting skills—thank you for all your great work! Many thanks to the sales, marketing, and publicity teams at Random House; I so appreciate all you do!

Thank you to my agent, Andy McNicol at William Morris Endeavor, who encouraged me to write *Timeless* back when I first came up with the idea and quickly found it a home with Random House. You changed my life in the best way! Special thanks also to my foreign rights agent, Laura Bonner, and my film agent, Eric Reid.

So many thanks to Heather Holley and Rob Hoffman for your incredible musical production on "I Remember." Recording with you guys was an amazing experience, and I'm grateful for your contribution to the world of *Timekeeper*!

Colleen Houck, thank you for your wonderful support and blurb; I'm honored! And thanks for all the awesome things you do for the YA community.

Michael Pietrocarlo, you are a truly great artist and friend. Thank you so much for bringing my vision of the Time Society Headquarters to life with your fantastic map illustration!

Kelly Rutherford, thank you so much for your enthusiasm and support of *Timeless*. Ann Marie Sanderlin, I so appreciate your passion for this project.

Brooke Kaufman-Halsband, thanks for all your love and for believing in me when I cold-called you at seventeen years old! Thanks also to everyone at HK Management.

To all the foreign publishers of the Timeless series, thank you for introducing my books to new audiences and making it possible for them to be read in other languages!

So many thanks to all the booksellers, librarians, bloggers, teachers, and everyone in the book community who helped get the word out about this series. I truly appreciate your enthusiasm and support!

I'm forever grateful for the best parents in the world, who

made all of this possible: my father, Shon Saleh (who inspired the character of Irving Henry!), and my mom, ZaZa Saleh. I love you both so much.

ZaZa, aka Mommy, you are my best friend and my guardian angel on earth! You've always championed my dreams, and while I wrote this book you outdid yourself with your kindness and generosity. From being my beta reader extraordinaire to whisking me off on a writing trip when I was under a deadline, you've been the most incredible support, and I am truly blessed!

A huge thank-you and lots of love to my spectacular big brother, Arian Saleh. Your thoughtful, intelligent feedback was so helpful and pushed me to make this story the best it could be. And thank you for introducing me to the books, movies and songs that have spurred on my creativity ever since we were little.

So much of being a writer is having a rich personal life to draw from, and that leads me to a very special acknowledgment. Thank you to my ♥, Chris Robertiello, for always making me laugh, giving me butterflies, bringing the greatest people into my life, and making every day feel like a wonderful adventure!

Thank you to James and Dorothy Robertiello for all the kindness, laughter and special times. Jimmy, I feel so lucky to have known you and will always remember the way you lived every day with love.

Lisa Kay, thank you for your beautiful spirit and for sharing your gifts with the world. The character of Elizabeth Jade in this book is inspired by you!

Chessa Latifi and Ross Donaldson, I'll never forget those summer days staying at your beach house while I brainstormed this book. Chessa, thank you for being a trusty beta reader and like a sister to me. Ross, thanks for the great writing advice, invaluable technology help during the crucial editing stages—and letting me turn your ancestor into a Timekeeper!

Josh Bratman, thank you for all your great feedback and support of my writing, and for inspiring me to include *Handbook of the Time Society* excerpts in this book. Lots of love to you, Alex, and the whole Bratman clan!

Mia Antonelli, ever since we started our epic instant-messenger chats eleven years ago, I knew that I'd found a best friend for life! Thank you for being such a wonderful, supportive friend throughout the years.

Sainaz Mokhtari—soon to be sister-in-law!—thank you for your great friendship and support of my projects.

Christina Harmon, thank you for bringing so much light into my life, and for all your sweet enthusiasm about the Timeless books. I appreciate you and your Chris so much!

Endless amounts of love to my Saleh and Madjidi grandparents and relatives across the globe; I'm so grateful for you all!

Thanks and love to awesome, supportive friends Camilla Moshayedi, Dan Kiger and Heather Williams, Jon and Emily Sandler, Marise Freitas, and Stacie Surabian.

To the Ameri, Cohanim, and McCartt families, thank you for believing in me since I was the little kid autographing your fence and insisting that we write and film movies at every one of our playdates. ☺

And of course, thanks to a doggie so special, she brings miracles everywhere she goes: Honey, you are the sweetest companion!

In memory of Monir Vakili, who left an incredible legacy that inspires me every day.

Continue reading to discover
how Michele and Philip's epic love story began
with an excerpt from Alexandra's first novel,

*Timeless*

1

Michele stood alone in the center of a hall of mirrors. The glass revealed a girl identical to Michele, with the same chestnut hair, ivory skin, and hazel eyes; even wearing the same outfit of dark denim jeans and black tank top. But when Michele moved forward, the girl in the glass remained still. And while Michele's own neck was bare, the reflection in the mirror wore a strange key hanging from a gold chain, a key unlike anything Michele had ever seen.

It was a gold skeleton key in a shape similar to a cross, but with a circular bow at the top. The image of a sundial was carved into the bow. The key looked weathered and somehow wise, as though it weren't inanimate, but a living being with over a century's worth of stories to share. Michele was momentarily seized by an urge to reach through the glass and touch the curious key. But all she felt was the cool surface of the mirror, and the girl with Michele's face betrayed no notice of her.

"Who are you?" Michele whispered. But the mirror image didn't respond, didn't even appear to have heard. Michele shivered nervously, and squeezed her eyes shut. What was this?

And then, suddenly, the silence was broken. Someone was whistling, a slow melody that created goose bumps on the back of Michele's neck. Her eyes snapped open, and she watched in shock as someone joined the girl in the mirror. Michele's breath caught in her throat. She felt paralyzed, unable to do anything but stare at him through the glass.

His eyes were such a deep blue they seemed to dazzle against his contrasting thick dark hair. Eyes the color of sapphires. And though she could somehow tell that he was around her age, he was dressed like none of the other boys she knew. He wore a crisp white collared shirt under a white silk vest and tie, formal black pants, and black patent leather shoes. In his white-gloved hands, he held a black top hat lined with silk. The formal clothing suited him. He was more than good-looking, much more than could be conveyed by the word "handsome." Michele felt an unfamiliar ache as she watched him.

Her heart racing, she stared at him as he carelessly peeled off his gloves and dropped his hat, the three items falling together in a heap on the floor. He then reached for the hand of the girl in the mirror. And to Michele's astonishment, she felt his touch. She quickly looked down, but though her hand was empty, she could feel his fingers interlacing with hers, the sensation causing a flutter inside her.

What's happening to me? Michele thought frantically. But

*suddenly she couldn't think anymore, for as she looked at the boy and girl embracing in the mirror, she felt strong arms encircling her own waist.*

*"I'm waiting for you," he murmured, smiling a slow, familiar grin that seemed to hint at a secret between them.*

*And for the first time, Michele and the mirror reflection were in sync as they both whispered, "Me too."*

Michele Windsor awoke with a shock, gasping for breath. As she took in the sight of her darkened bedroom, her heartbeat slowed and she remembered—it was just The Dream. The same strange, intoxicating dream that had haunted her on and off for years. As always, waking up from it brought the pain of disappointment into the pit of Michele's stomach, as she found herself missing him—this person who didn't even exist.

She'd been just a little girl when she'd first begun dreaming of him, so young that she hadn't yet resembled the teenager in the mirror. The dreams were infrequent then; they came just once or twice a year. But as she grew up, looking like the twin of the girl in the mirror, the dreams began to flood her consciousness with a new urgency, as if they were trying to *tell* her something. Michele frowned as she slumped back against her pillows, wondering if she would ever understand. But then, Confusion and Mystery had been principal players in her life since the day she was born.

Michele rolled over onto her side, facing her bedroom window, and listening to the waves lapping the shore outside the Venice Beach bungalow. The sound usually lulled her to sleep quickly, but not that night. She couldn't seem to get those sapphire eyes out of her head. Eyes that she had practically memorized, without ever having seen them in her waking life.

*"See that I'm everywhere, everywhere, shining down on you . . ."*

The pulsing hip-hop beat of the Lupe Fiasco song "Shining Down" blared from Michele's iPod alarm the next morning. She unearthed her head from the covers and pressed the Snooze button. How could it already be morning? It felt like just moments earlier that she had managed to fall back to sleep.

"Michele!" a voice sang out from across the hall. "Are you up? I made pancakes, come eat them before they get cold."

Michele's eyes flickered open. Sleep or pancakes? That was a no-brainer. Her mouth was already beginning to water at the thought of her mom's specialty. She threw on a robe and fuzzy slippers and padded through the modest house until she reached the cozy kitchen. Marion Windsor was in her usual morning mode, sipping coffee while studying her newest clothing designs in her sketchbook. The crinkly sound of Marion's favorite old jazz record, by none other than her grandmother Lily Windsor, echoed from their vintage record player.

"Good morning, sweetie," Marion greeted her daughter, looking up from her sketchbook with a smile.

"Morning." Michele leaned over to give her mom a kiss and glanced at the sketch she'd been working on. A long, flowing dress with a bit of a Pocahontas-circa-2010 feel, it was right in keeping with the other bohemian-chic pieces in her mom's line, Marion Windsor Designs.

"I like it," Michele said approvingly. She settled into her seat in front of a plate of golden pancakes topped with strawberries. "And *this*, I definitely like."

"*Bon appétit.*" Marion grinned. "Speaking of food, do you have lunch plans with the girls today?"

Michele shrugged as she inhaled her first forkful of delicious pancake. "Just the usual, nothing special."

"Well, I have a free afternoon, so I was thinking I could pick you up at lunch and we could go for burgers at Santa Monica Pier," Marion suggested. "What do you say?"

Michele gave her mom a sideways look. "You still feel sorry for me, don't you?"

"What? No!" Marion said innocently.

Michele raised an eyebrow at her.

"Okay, fine," Marion said, relenting. "I don't feel *sorry* for you, because I know you're so much better off without him. But I can't stand to see you hurt."

Michele nodded, looking away. It had been two weeks since her first real boyfriend, Jason, had broken up with her on the eve of the first day of school. His exact words had been "Babe, you know I think you're the best and all, but it's my senior year and I can't have the baggage of a relationship. I gotta live it up, play the field. You get it, right?" *Uh, not exactly.* So Michele had to begin her junior year with a broken heart, which grew all the more painful last week, when word spread that Jason was hooking up with a sophomore, Carly Marsh.

Marion reached across the table and squeezed Michele's

hand. "Sweetie, I know how hard it is to see your first boy-friend with someone else. It's just going to take a little time to heal from this."

"But really, I *should* be over it," Michele vented. "I mean, all he ever talked about was water polo, and he was about as romantic as a toothpick. I just really miss—I don't know. . . ."

"That butterflies-in-your-stomach feeling of wanting to be with someone, and knowing they feel the same way about you?" Marion guessed.

"Yeah," Michele admitted sheepishly. "Exactly."

"Well, I can promise that you'll have that again, but with someone so much better," Marion said intently.

"How do you know that?" Michele asked doubtfully.

"Because we mothers have an intuition about these things. So when you see Jason with Carly, do your best to just shrug it off and think how lucky you are to be free for a guy who's actually worthy of you."

Michele shook her head wonderingly. It never ceased to amaze her that her mom had such an optimistic outlook on Michele's love life—or even still *believed* in love—after all Marion herself had been through in that department.

"I'm serious," Marion insisted. "And in the meantime, are you using all this as fodder for your writing?"

"Oh, you know it," Michele said wryly. "Lots of angsty song lyrics and poems."

"That's my girl," Marion encouraged. "You'd better let me read some of it soon."

"Once I edit everything down to perfection? Sure," Michele said with a grin. "And I think I will take you up on burgers at the beach."

Even though she was more than a little skeptical of Marion's predictions about her love life, Michele always felt better after confiding in her. It had been the two of them against the world since Michele was born, and there was never a problem or a heartache that Marion couldn't fix with her stubborn resolve and humor.

"Honey, you're looking pretty pale," Marion noticed, eyeing her with concern. "Did you sleep well last night?"

"Not really. I woke up in the middle of the night after dreaming about Mystery Man, and then it took me forever to fall back to sleep."

"So you saw him again," Marion said, her eyes lighting up. "Do tell."

"Mom, I know you think the dreams are cool and all, but I can never meet this guy in real life," Michele reminded her. "So the whole thing is actually really irritating."

"Well, I think it's romantic. Maybe it's your subconscious telling you not to worry about Jason, that you *will* find someone special." Marion glanced at her watch. "Yikes, it's seven-thirty! You'd better go get ready."

"Okay, I'll be back in fifteen." Michele hurried to her room and changed into a fitted white tee, Abercrombie jeans with a skinny metallic belt, and a pair of black flats. She quickly ran a brush through her hair and dabbed on some concealer and lip gloss before tossing the three beauty essentials into her messenger bag.

Michele found Marion waiting in their Volvo outside the bungalow. As they set off toward Santa Monica, Marion flicked on the CD player. "I want you to hear my latest discovery," she said. "Well, maybe that's not the most accurate description, since she's a Grammy-winning artist who's been around for decades. But I only recently heard about her, and she just might be my new favorite singer—after my grandmother, of course."

Michele curiously waited for the music to start. Her mom had such eclectic taste she never knew what to expect. This music surprised her. It managed to be heavy and light all at once, both breezy and aching. As soon as she heard the opening chords of the two Spanish guitars and the swaying Brazilian rhythm, Michele felt like she was transported to an exotic paradise. But when a woman with a deep, husky voice began to sing in Portuguese a melody rich with minor keys, Michele instantly knew that she was singing about pain. And yet the song wasn't sad, exactly.

"Nostalgia," Marion explained. "That word she keeps singing, *sodade*—it's the Portuguese word for a nostalgia so intense we don't have a direct translation for it in English."

"Wow." Michele picked up the CD case and looked at the cover photo of the singer, who appeared to be in her sixties or seventies. Her name was Cesaria Evora. Michele and her mom listened to the rest of the song in silence, and as the final chords played, Michele asked, "What does it make you think of?"

Marion paused. "Home," she said so quietly that Michele almost wondered if she had misheard.

She stared at her mom. "Really?"

But they had just pulled up in front of her school, Crossroads High. Marion didn't answer; she just smiled at Michele and smoothed back her daughter's hair. "See you at lunch, honey."

"Bye, Mom." Michele gave her a quick hug. "Love you."

"I love you too. Good luck with—you know." Marion gave her a meaningful smile before zooming off, her long auburn hair flying behind her.

Turn the page to read an
original *Timekeeper* short story,

*The Message*

## MANHATTAN
APRIL 19, 1912

Philip James Walker kept his head down as the voices in the Peacock Alley foyer rose to a new high, bursting the private bubble of his piano playing. He moved his hands across the keys automatically, performing like the dutiful hotel pianist he was. But for the first time in his life, music failed to fill the empty space inside him. His mind and emotions were elsewhere—lost in the freezing Atlantic, along with the last family member he truly loved.

Philip's fingers struck a dissonant note as he pictured his cousin Herbert's exuberant face. He'd been like a little brother to Philip, a fixture in his most vital memories. Philip's father used to take the two boys on regular weekend outings—on sailing trips, to softball games, out for ice cream sundaes—and when he died, Herbie was the one who'd stood by Philip's side at the funeral, too young to know what to say, yet better able to comfort him than anyone else. He was even there on that life-altering day in Newport when Philip caught his first glimpse of Michele. But now, all that remained of him was a boldfaced name in a horror story covered by all the papers: "Fifteen-Year-Old Walker Company Heir Herbert Louis Walker Among *Titanic*'s 1,500 Dead."

Philip was reminded of something Michele once said, before she left his Time. *"Why do I have to say goodbye to everyone I love?"* Nowadays, he often asked himself the very same thing.

He stared at the keys, daring himself to stop playing. *Get up! Turn your back on these Fifth Avenue fools arguing senselessly about the ship. You don't belong here.* But though he loathed himself for it, he remained in place. Now that his mother and stepfather had cut him off from his inheritance, Philip couldn't afford to lose his job. It was a small miracle that he was even able to afford his one-room studio downtown; without work, he would find himself out on the street.

"Excuse me, sir?"

Philip glanced up at the sound of a man's voice, expecting to find one of the regulars from the nearby gentlemen's clubs, requesting he play the latest rag. But to Philip's surprise, the man was both unexpected and familiar. He remembered that kind smile, just as he remembered those haunted eyes and the slight stoop of his walk. It was his family's old lawyer, Irving Henry of Washington Square. Philip hadn't seen him in years.

"Hello, Mr. Henry."

As they shook hands across the piano, Philip found that he couldn't look away. There was something about the man's face that was more than simply familiar. He *resembled* someone. . . . Philip shook his head, brushing the thought aside. His constant dreaming of Michele was manifesting itself again, causing him to see her face everywhere he looked.

"Philip Walker." Irving's expression warmed as he looked at Philip. "I'm sorry, I didn't mean to interrupt. But, well, it's a relief to find a friendly face on a day like this."

"I'm a friendly face, then?" Philip managed a grin. "You haven't seen me since I was in boarding school breeches."

"You're more of a friend than you know. Especially compared to what's behind that door." Irving nodded toward the East Room, at the other end of the Waldorf-Astoria hotel lobby.

Philip felt the block of ice return to his stomach.

"The *Titanic* hearings . . . So you're one of the lawyers on the case?"

"I'm assisting Senator Smith with the investigation. And I can promise you, Philip, the White Star Line will be held accountable for this tragedy." Irving met Philip's gaze. "I'm awfully sorry about Herbert. He was a fine boy."

Philip swallowed the lump in his throat. "He was the only family I had left. I wish it had been me instead. Then I could have seen Michele again—"

Philip clapped a hand over his mouth, shocked by his own outburst. He had never spoken Michele's name to anyone else. She was his secret. But Herbie's death had frayed his nerves, and now he was slipping, no longer choosing his words carefully the way he used to. And there was something about Irving . . . something that, strangely, made him *want* to talk.

"Oh, but she's here," said the older man.

Philip's head snapped up.

"What? What did you say?"

"Your Michele." Irving smiled softly. "She's here, and she exists everywhere you were together."

Philip opened his mouth to speak, but no words came. How—*how* could Irving know what he was talking about? How did he even know who Michele was? Or . . . was Irving simply reciting platitudes, assuming Philip was mourning a lost love from their own, linear timeline? Before he could ask further, a short, stout man carrying a file of papers appeared at Irving's elbow.

"It's starting, Mr. Henry," he said grimly.

"Did you hear that, ladies?" a lavishly dressed matron cried to her tea companions. "The inquiry is starting. Hurry, I don't want to miss a minute of the show!"

Philip bit down on his lip to keep the angry retort from escaping. Fifteen hundred people had died, and yet so many of those untouched by the tragedy were treating it like a Shakespearean play put on for their own amusement. *"Who will they pin the blame on—the chairman, or the architect? And who do you suppose Madeleine Astor will go for now that poor old Jack is dead?"* If Philip overheard one more of these careless comments tossed about in the hotel, his already-shot nerves would snap.

Irving glared at the woman, then placed a gentle hand on Philip's shoulder.

"Would the boss mind if you took a break? Lord knows you've been through a shock these past few days."

Philip glanced at the thinning crowd in the foyer. Women in elaborate hats and furs were making their way toward the

East Room, their skirts swishing behind them, as top-hatted gentlemen followed at a more languid pace. No one would miss him or his piano. But the inquiry was the last place he wished to be.

"Thank you, Mr. Henry. And good luck in there," Philip said, shaking the lawyer's hand.

"And to you, young man," Irving said. "Remember . . . you're never quite alone."

Philip watched him go, his brow furrowed in confusion. What did Irving mean by his odd remarks?

He walked slowly through the sumptuous corridors of the Waldorf, so similar to the chillingly perfect palace that was his former home, Walker Mansion. With all the hotel's occupants either crammed inside the East Room or huddled outside the door, Philip had the halls to himself. And he knew just where he would go.

Philip rounded the bend and quickened his pace, until he was standing at the door to the hotel ballroom. He hadn't been inside since the Vanderbilt Ball nearly two years ago, when Michele had visited his Time and they'd shared a dance and a kiss that he'd relived over and over in his mind since.

He opened the door. Daylight streamed through the windows, and aside from the shadows dancing across the parquet floor, Philip was alone. He moved through the emptiness to the corner he had once shared with Michele. To his astonishment, he felt a warm pressure against his hand.

Surely he had only imagined it? After all, he was the sole person in the ballroom. But as he opened his palm . . . a slip of *paper* fluttered to the floor, paper that he certainly hadn't been holding before. His heart hammering in his chest, Philip quickly retrieved the note and began to read.

*I'm with you in a whole other place and time.*

*The world has light.*

*I come to life.*

For a moment, Philip could scarcely breathe. Those were *Michele's* words, from the song they had written together—and this was her handwriting.

"Michele?" he whispered, daring to hope that she might materialize in front of him again, after all this time.

He felt a sigh on the back of his neck and he spun around, his pulse racing with anticipation. But still no one else was in the room. And yet, Philip *knew* she was near. How else could he have received this message?

The parquet floor creaked, as if bearing the weight of footsteps. Philip took a few steps toward the sound and held out his hand. He might have looked alone, but he wasn't. He could feel her small, smooth fingers interlacing his. She was here, in this very room—*but in her own Time.* They were together even while they were apart.

*"Remember . . . you're never quite alone."*

Irving's words echoed in Philip's ears, and he felt a smile spread across his face. It was true. Michele was reminding him of it this very minute. One hundred years separated them, but they could still hear each other, feel each other. He might have lost the people he loved most, but only on the linear, physical plane. They still surrounded him; they lived on in their own Time.

"I'm not alone," Philip murmured. "I can do this. I can survive and make something of myself . . . just like you believed I would. Your love will keep me going, Michele."

Philip felt a soft pressure encircling him, and he sensed it was her arms—a century away, but holding him nonetheless. He would walk through those doors a different man, now that she had reminded him that anything was possible. That a love like this kept people alive.

And Philip's love would lift and carry him through the dark, into the light.

APRIL 19, 2014

Michele Windsor stared at the scrap of paper as it fluttered from her hands to the floor. What had possessed her to do what she just did, and in the middle of a tour group, no less?

Dorothy Windsor held on to Michele's arm, hobbling slightly as they moved forward. It pained Michele to see how her grandmother had aged over the past two years, and she wondered if this much exertion was a good idea. But Dorothy had insisted on attending the Waldorf-Astoria's brand-new historical tour.

As the tour progressed, Michele realized that Dorothy hadn't wanted to learn about the hotel's history—she wanted to *remember* it. Many of the twentieth-century galas and balls their guide waxed poetic about had been attended by Dorothy herself, and she whispered her recollections into Michele's ear as they visited each room. They had just finished hearing about the harrowing *Titanic* investigation held at the hotel a century ago, and now they were in the historic ballroom. Michele was tempted to whisper a recollection of her own to her grandmother: *"I was here in 1910. I danced in this very room with the boy I loved."*

That was when Michele felt him, and was compelled to pull a pen and notepad from her purse and—strange as it may sound—write him. And now, as Dorothy said, "Dear, you dropped something," Michele pretended not to hear. She watched the paper intently, her eyes filled with hope. And then . . . it happened. The paper disappeared.

Michele gasped, her eyes brimming with tears at the realization that Philip had received her message, one hundred years in the past. The Time Society was right.

Her abilities were only just beginning.

Excerpt copyright © 2014 by Alexandra Monir.
Published by Ember, an imprint of Random House
Children's Books, a division of Random House LLC,
a Penguin Random House Company, New York.

Find out how Michele discovered her ability
to time travel in the digital
original short story,

*Secrets of
the Time Society*

# ABOUT THE AUTHOR

Alexandra Monir broke into the world of YA novels with her debut, *Timeless*. She is a singer/songwriter and recorded original music to accompany both *Timeless* and *Timekeeper*, her second novel. She lives in Los Angeles. Check out alexandra monir.com for music and more!